ANONYMOUS

A True Life Story of Sex, Lies and Deception and How To Spot:
When The Other Woman Is NOT A Woman!

RON GARRETT

Anonymous Publishing

ISBN: 978-0-578-26755-5

PRINTED IN THE UNITED STATES OF AMERICA

WARNING: This book is broken out into two sections in each chapter there is a Chapter and a Story. The Story section is XXX Rated and Chapter 1 is XXX also. You can read the entire book without the XXX Rated stories if you want just the information. I will mark each section with XXX so you are not subject to something you are not interested in. The names have been changed to protect identity. But all stories are true and factually correct.

TABLE OF CONTENTS

PROLOGUE

-**XXX**-

And then it happened the door next to me closed and my heart raced. Trying to see who it was when my eyes had not adjusted for the darkness. But who was I kidding, what they looked like really didn't matter at that point. I slide my index finger in a quarter circle pattern through a four inch hole that had been put at a perfect height. And then what I waited for all day and night, I could hear the pants unzip. The anticipation overwhelming me, thinking "what will it be"? What piece of wonderful was going to appear through the four inch circle. How big? What Color? Clean or smelly.? One never knows and depending on the day would it be rejected? No matter how much I want it, I was careful not to ever do smelly, unclean or in anyway suspicious looking or feeling cocks. After all I had standards just not many. Sometimes I was surprised and many times not in a good way.

Let me start from the beginning of the day.

As the excitement builds within me I am totally feeling flushed and overwhelmed. I was a restaurant owner and had to do a lot of running to pick up product and this day was no different. from any others but this day I had allowed myself a extra hour and a half of free time. I said "Linda can you do any orders that may coming in I have to get to the Aurora Packing so I can get back for the dinner shift" Linda " sure I doubt if there will be anything much anyway." But to cover myself I had made sure that this day I would have an extra cook come in to work the evening shift just incase my day got really fun.

It was a typical day, everyday really when I tried to get away from the restaurant with a thousand questions from everyone. But I hurried and would run out the door for the excitement of an-other Anonymous or if I were lucky a couple Anonymous guys. My pulse grew ever faster as I raced out to the car where I kept a dif-ferent shirt. As I drove, removing my chef coat and put on a regular shirt. I got away, but not nearly as often as I wanted, or should I say needed.

Traveling down route 30, I pulled up behind the building about 35 minutes away from the restaurant that I owned. Hurrying out of the car grabbing five dollar and seeing the non responsive clerk with my head down I gave the clerk the money and scurried away. Walking between rows of x-rated movies entering the back dark video arcade through a black curtain trying not to be seen and de-fiantly not ever making eye contact with anyone. The arcade area was basically a square of hallways with booths on both sides, the middle island the booths were a bit bigger.

I made one loop around the square of booths to see who was there lurking in the dark. But I knew I could not waste time so I picked one booth locked the door and waited. As I sat there I real-ized this was the booth with glory holes on both sides. This was the time that was always the most intense when inside me the desire would overcome me and excruciating anticipation almost painful. There was always a porn movie of some-kind playing but hardly never watched.

I sat in the dark wondering what husband would walk in the

other sided. Did I know them? Were they just having lunch at my place? Did they come in my bar? Honestly I really didn't care. And then it happened the door next to me opened, closed and locked then my heart raced. Trying to see who it was what they looked like but it really didn't matter at that point. I slide my index finger in a quarter circle through a four inch circular hole that had been put at a perfect height. And then the glorious moment happened, what I waited all day and night for, I could hear the pants unzip and me thinking what will it be. Through the hole appeared the head of a beautiful thick piece of manhood in all it glory. Within inches of my mouth, touching it and then smelling my fingers to assure it was clean and started licking and sucking like I was on a deserted island and this was my first water in weeks. It grew and enjoying it more than I should, all my worries, concerns and thoughts of what is happening was wrong escaped me.

It was now just me and him in a world an underground world of man on man lust. Not love just the male instinct to desire an **Anonymous**. Working on him for about five minutes I knew by the sounds and the movement that he was ready to explode in all his glory. I was not and still am not a swallower, but many are, just not my thing. The pace picked up and finished jacking him shooting his load which hit the wall of the other side of the stall. His moan was loud but quick. And I sat there wondering what wife will not get any tonight. As quickly as he appeared he was gone the unknown face in a small cubical just outside of Aurora Illinois was a pleasant memory. Now franticly wanting more I looked at my watch and had ten more minutes and then would have to leave. OMG my lucky day the door next to me closed again and repeating the same motion a quarter circle with a index finger (the universal motion that tells the other **Anonymous** you want it) but this time I was met with another finger so I quickly stood up from the folding chair almost knocking it over in excitement. Undid my pants and slid my erect manhood through the hole of glory and in total joy of the gentleness and warmth of the mouth who obviously enjoyed me as much as I enjoyed others. Suddenly out of nowhere I exploded into his mouth and he wanted it all. He would not let go he kept sucking I knew he was one of us, the truly **Anonymous**.

Bending over and through the four inch hole I said thanks, like I was buying a ticket at the movie theater. I suddenly realized that while my cock was being serviced there was another one behind me sticking through with full erection. And what a beauty it was approximately 8 inches extremely thick as a matter of fact I was afraid he was so thick he was stuck till he came. Like male dog that swelled inside the bitch and had to cum to get off. The veins were beautiful even though once I cum normally I loose all interest this was to big and beautiful to pass up. I sucked him with all my might and he moaning like an injured wild animal. I looked at my watch and it had been fifteen minutes in my mouth and no sign of cumming. I knew this was going to be worth the effort so I was a bit more aggressive than normal because of the rock hard meat and then it happen the veins started bulging and the time was near. I got him very wet and started jacking him and the eruption happened he was so hard and stiff he shot directly through the other hole with three pulses that anyone watching would have gotten a real face full.

This is my Story and how I became (or always was) bi or gay not big on labels but something like that, ...and it just maybe your story but you don't know it. If you are a married female and reading this you......

Are you starting to think there there maybe another woman things are not just right?

There is something different but you can't put your finger on it?

Well the Other Woman just maybe another Man or more correctly many other men.....It can happen to anyone, anyone. Some would say my wife and I were "The perfect couple", they have everything going for them, wow to be so successful at an early age. Thats what we heard all the time. If they only knew. If they only had one idea that I was an **Anonymous**.........cock sucker.

1

"HOW IT ALL STARTED"

− XXX −

Let's take a look back at how I began my journey into the world of Bi/Gay Sexually. As with most straight people it starts with a fantasy about being with the same sex. Then that fantasy progresses many times by experimenting with their lover, husband, wife etc. And for most they will never move any farther that the interaction with the spouse. At least that is what we tell ourselves and our spouses or partners. But the reality is that this desire started much younger in life and because of social norms we hide our desires, fantasies and some say perversions. I can not remember when my thoughts first started but the rocky road into right and wrong, as others see it, has stayed with me up to this day.

I was about 13-14 years old as memory serves me when I created in my head a female lover who would take care of my thoughts about having sex for the first time. She was the sister of the two guys that lived next to me but they did not have a sister. This Fantasy lover became real to me, so real in fact the I would tell my best friend James exactly what she would do to me and for me.

And as my stories became more and more detailed and as we got older, freshman into high school I needed them to come true. But being an overweight, and not particularly better than average looking, the reality was that I would not or could not find a female to fill my desires. So the more I told James my stories the more I wanted to act out and have them come true so one evening when I was spending the night at his house I started my stories but this time I really wanted it! So I told James a virgin also, maybe we could do what she does to me, to each other. He was very nervous and so was I but we started by slowing feeling the others balls and cock. Both of us started to get hard and that meant to me that we both enjoyed it. So I told him that since I was experienced "Let me show you what she does to me," "Well if you are sure you want to I guess it would be ok." James said. So slowly making my way under the covers to find his extremely hard cock, started licking it and was not particularly fond of the taste. But not wanting to kill the moment I continued, having his entire member in my mouth, as my fantasy is coming true for the first time, he started to make loud noises. Shhhhhh you will wake everyone up." With in a minute or two of the total pleasing of servicing my first cock he said he was cumming and cum he did! I did not let him cum in my mouth (which is something even to this day I try not to let happen). He shot the biggest load I had ever seen it just kept pulsating and at that moment I knew that I would not be a swallower. Remembering the only load I had ever seen was mine.

Moving up next to him and said "told you it would feel good." At that point it was my turn to get the pleasure for the truly first time. He was not as enthusiastic as I was but as I would learn later once a guy cums he is less likely to give anyone else pleasure. Something in our physical and psychological make up I guess. Many males have a desire to be totally satisfied without concern of their partner but we do a good job of acting. No matter what they say it is all about them. The only reason they go through the motions of satisfying their lover is so they get it more and more often. But James tried and did take it in his mouth a worked me over for a minute or two till I said OMG I am cumming and he moved and I shot an equally impressive load. Thick, Creamy and satisfying. Then like robots we both got up went to the bathroom and washed off. Went to bed and said well now we both know how it will feel when we find the right girl. We agreed it was great and glad the experiment was over, he more than me as memory serves me. This same thing would happen each time I spent the night up on the hill in Channahon Illinois.

And each time I had to make the fantasy with the neighbors sister more and more intriguing so I could convince him there was something new to show him. As memory serves we did this about five times and then life happened and we were getting too old to be boyish trisks it would be moving to be Gay or find a real Girl Friend. So we went the way of the established norm or what is perceived as normal in society, well at least in the sixties.

There was another time we were on a family camping trip and another friend Donnie was there sleeping in the back of at the camper which was nothing more than an old yellow school bus that my father had so proudly converted to a camper. He spent every waking hour working on this bus building everything by hand. Yes we were the true Tennessee Hillbilly's living in the north the ones we secretly laugh at today. And I am not being judgmental of others just telling the truth we tend to be very judgmental of people that are not like us, that don't believe like us. I am Honestly not saying this is right it just is. And even as I am writing it sounds so wrong. And maybe this will help in pre-judging from this moment forward.

May this be the moment we truly realize when we put anyone down or make comments about them it is judgment that is totally unnecessary. Well something to think about for my next book.

But in all honesty now in looking back the homemade camper never embarrassed me when I was younger because I had not learned how to have prejudice in life or about life. My Father had a best friend who was black and this was totally out of the norm in the fifties and sixties. He would use the "N" word but only when Gaven was around and I always found it peculiar. My Father was a damn civil rights leader, at a time when only gutless politcians trying to pander to minories acted like they carried about others for a goddamn vote. My dad truly cared about everyone.

In looking back at our situation we never understood what the business men that wore suit and tie living next to us thought. And now we live in a world, where it's only ok to put your own type down otherwise its racist, homophobic, xenophobic, or what ever phobia you want to add here, we accept it. But as I truly think about it is it really ok? Can you truly say Nigger if you are black to another black person? Can you say Fag to a gay guy if you are gay? Or should you? Doesn't that give everyone else equal liberties to say it too? That question has always perplexed me WHY is it ok? Why is it because we all have an internal desire to somehow put others down? Is it passive aggressive? It maybe just in fun (so we say) but is it really? This brings me to a bigger question are we all hiding something? Most of the time true feeling come out accidentally by a comment that was not suppose to sound as truthful as it did. I know that also many times we make comments out of frustration and not really our intent. Most of us never tell anyone about our prejudices because we know it is wrong. In all my years I am not sure how or why we came to hate like we have. I feel bad ever thinking past thoughts but that should not define who I am now. This Wok society is killing us where no matter what we are judged. Judge me now not in the past if we can not grow and learn as a society then where will we end up.

Back to Donnie. The families were camping and as boys of that age alway do telling each other to suck my cock never truly meaning it just boys being boys. But one night in the back of the camper which was designed with four bunk beds two on each side with a narrow walkway in between. Donnie was joking but telling me to suck his cock. I said no but he got down from the top bunk and put his cock only an inch from my face and started stroking it. Even though I could see it I asked where are you I can't see it is too dark. I did not want to do anything with him because he had a big mouth and for sure would tell others. But O how I wanted to go down on it suck him like I was sure he had never been sucked by anyone. But I rejected my desires of my big mouth friend. So I let him jack it again I said " where are you it is so dark I can't see a thing?" knowing all the time his big cock was a few inches from my face. Then he laughed got on the top bunk and said "I had it almost in your mouth," We laughed and I said no way I did not even see you.

From that point on nothing else happened for a few years I recessed my feeling to have a hard pulsing cock in my mouth and went to the "normal" side of life. But never loosing the desire and fantasy about being with another guy. Always in the back of my head I knew, I truly knew.

As with everything in life that becomes a pattern there is a beginning normally there is not an end. Unless we consider death the ultimate end. We continue with our mundane life going on day to day not being happy, not being sad just being. Last evening I was watching the interview with Adel that Oprah had and many things about life became clearer. (Side note how is it that some people in the world only need a first name and everyone understands who we are talking about. And two of them were on TV together.) She was commenting about her divorce and how she realized playing a sort of truth or dare game with two friends. The question came up what is one thing that know one knows about you? Her answer without thinking was I am not happy in her marriage. Well it sounds like this stunned her friends and it was the first time she had said it out loud. With all her money and fame Adel was not happy. Even though she says she loves her former husband till this day she was not in love with him. And nothing sums up that's exactly how Bi/Gay people feel in a straight marriage. More about that in an upcoming chapters.

As a young adolescent we all fantasize about sex, what is it? How do we do it? With whom will I do it? To the best of my recollection mine fascination with sex was finding paperback novels in a high shelf in the bathroom of our house. Being an only child and did not have any older siblings to ask questions so I had to find everything out on my own. My dad who honestly never thought of as a reader had the books in the bathroom where I assume he would go in private with out mom knowing. He did spend a lot of time in there somedays.

The first time I found them I started reading and my excitement grew. So when I told my best friend James about it and then began the start of my lying and sexual fascination that leads up to my lying life as a husband and father.

In telling James the stores from the book I decided to make the stories my stories so I started telling him my fantasy as if they were real. I made up this story knowing that we could live a fantasy together we were best friends and I truly wanted to take the journey with him so I thought.As my made up girl next door was the catalyst to all my stories, I would tell him how an older girl next door that obviously did not exist would come over and teach me about sex. In turn I could help James understand strictly as a mentor don't you know. In reading the paperbacks I had a good idea of how to tell the story to him. And thus as I told the story my imaginary girl next door gave me my first sexual experience with my best friend. I guess you could say that books caused me to become more curious and took my path to this book.

As we take this journey together now in reading this book, I hold nothing back many of the pages that I write are not proud moments but they are real moments. And Real is were I am now and hope to always stay. This is a book of truths and I have intentionally not naming names and locations of my stories. And the names that I have used are not the real names this will help protect and one that is not invested in the book. This is not in any way a promotion of the Anonymous lifestyle it is just an honest depiction of real life that goes on every day.

STORY 1: COUPLE IN PORN ARCADE

–XXX–

The couple stood in the video booth doorway of my favorite, adult arcade/theaters, they were perfectly positioned at the T intersection, allowing them to see every guy that walked back and forth. Thus giving the husband and wife the opportunity to discuss which of them they were going to invite in their booth to play. Fred the husband was more than willing to let her always pick the guy but being the good wife Ann always wanted him to feel like he had a say. But we all know that he did not. As I walked by them I heard Ann say to her husband "lift my skirt and finger me till the perfect man walks by". Ann said it loud enough to obviously get my attention.

She was a gorgeous 40 year old with blond hair shoulder length and perfect dimensions. Curves that would make you take a second look and dressed for action. Breasts reveled almost to the nipples in her very low cut blue knit dress. It was the one that did not cover either shoulder and made her even sexier that she was already. It was a very large cinema and arcade. I felt this lady always knew she could control any man or woman there. In the cinema there was a choice of watching a movie on the large screen or giving a show to the multiple passersby of the private booth. Tonight she wanted the private booth and Fred knew what that meant. He was going to get used. Fred said "Ann your pussy is so wet" I know you are getting me ready for some lucky guy. "Yes dear what ever you want" he said. "There he is, I want him" Ann said. Keep an eye on him when he turns around and heads back this way call him over. Even though I heard every word I kept walking. Ok I will Fred said. As I started to walk by again Fred said hey how are you? Good thanks and you? Then Ann said "so what's your name? I am Ann and this is Fred."

"Ron, nice to meet you both". Ann said do you want to join us, as she rubbed my crotch. "Sure" I said upon entering the booth closing the door she came to me and started whispering in my ear. He likes to watch and be used are you ok with that? "Yes baby" I said as I kissed her in front of her husband she then looked at him said get to your knees and watch how a real man does it and learn this time.

I quickly had her tits out of the slinky off the shoulder blue dress and was sucking her nipples till they were so hard I thought they would squirt. Abruptly she got on the chair that was in the booth and forced my head into her warm wet pussy. I licked and ate it like I was starving. Totally had forgotten about the man on the floor watching us. Then with out asking she reached down unzipped my pants and my hard cock was exposed just inches from his face. I helped Ann down kissing her again and then she shoved my cock in her husband's waiting mouth. She said "get it wet bitch." As he was sucking me I bent her over the back of the chair and pulled out of his mouth and in one move slid all the way in her waiting pussy. This move caused a yelp that we were sure everyone could hear, but who cared at that point. Pumping her extremely hot and wet pussy, like it was our wedding night.

Engulfed in the beauty of the moment I realized this was the first lady I had ever I fucked or kissed other than my wife. She used her pussy like a vice grip contracting and releasing like a true pro. The repeated action caused me to cum much quicker that I ever wanted to but it felt so good I wanted it to go on forever. But my cock could not take it and she let out a moan she was cuming giving me a chance to let go also. She said are you ready to cum I said almost getting close. Take it out she yelled.

I pulled out she turned her head and said look at the bitch he wants more and again we made him take it in his mouth she said "suck it you fucking cunt." We were a little louder than we should be but could not stop. Then she whispered make me cum again so I pulled out of his mouth put it back in her waiting love pocket and continued pumping till she screamed holding on to both tits like I was riding a bronco. I gave her a huge white milky load. Turned her around and put my tongue deep in her mouth. We both calmed down and without a word she straddled her husband's open mouth and dropped the biggest cum load causing him to gag two times while swallowing it all. She make him lick her dry and put my limp dick in his mouth and cleaning me too. I sucked her tits again and she said go for a walk get ready for round two. I said "Really" o my god .

About 30 minutes later I walked by and she called me over. She told me that she was satisfied but he needed a little more abuse. So again we closed the door and he started to take his place on the floor but this time she asked me to bend over I did as instructed and she made him eat my ass like there was no tomorrow. I got instantly hard. Ok she said change position's I said not into that not you baby, you are going to fuck his lubed ass. I had never done that before not a girl or guy. But she got down and sucked me even harder and then glided me in to his gaping hole. I was so hard I went slow but she grabbed my ass and said show that fag who is in charge. I went balls deep in one motion. Causing him to let out a deep moan or yell could not tell the difference nor did I care. Ann said take it you bitch. You wanted to fuck my ass now you know what it feels like. As I pumped away on Freds ass making him feel every inch. Ann and I kissed and I sucked her tits again like a starving newborn. Finally he said he can't take any more, she told me harder fuck him harder. I slapped and pounded his ass red then I again exploded moaning she kissed me deep and told him to shut up. Then said pull out of him, I did as instructed she pushed Fred down and he took all my cock in his mouth cleaning me like a cat cleans her kittens. She then told him to leave the booth not even giving him time to pull up his pants. She and I finished making out while we heard guys talking to her husband then she opened the door and said to the two guys, I want you two to face fuck him now. We both stood with the door open husband on knees service two big cocks in the hallway as many other guys walked by. One came shooting all over his face while the other shot it down his throat. The whole time I am fingering Ann and sucking her firm tits. She laughed at her husband then bent over kissed him and looked at me saying thanks, great night see you again soon. But as faith would have it we never did. And that was the thing about Anonymous sex I didn't care. It was sex not love there will always be others. But I had a hell of a night.

2

THE EVENT THAT TURNED THE TIES TO OPEN BI/GAY

Well this is the story that converted me to Gay still Bi occasionally. It was mid July and my wife and I should have everything going for us retired, new house on the ocean a the tropical setting of Puerto Vallarta in a gated community. But not all things are as they seem. I was total miserable I hated my life and I hated feeling so bad all the time. My second wife was making fun of me laughing in a more than cruel manner. She had not worked in years, counting on me for everything but still biting the hand that was feeding her. I hate to make it sound like that but the truth is the truth.

And that is the way that marriages work give and take but when it came to her it was take and take and take some more, I had enough. So she was heading to spend more money in the USA visiting friends and seeing family which is a great thing because family is important to me more now than ever before. The week she and her cruelty left I had decided that I was getting a divorce. I had just finished my house in La Cruz Mexico it is located on the north side of the bay from Puerto Vallarta. I had designed and worked every day from start to finish with an architect/builder we built the house in exactly six months. Four bedrooms, theater room very very creative design. With a Chefs kitchen to die for, sixty four handles in the kitchen, nine by ten foot see through glass waterfall in the living room overlooking the pool another outside waterfall and pool area. To say it was my dream house would be an understatement. But I was willing to walk away and never see it again if I could only get away from her negativity.

Enough was enough from the utterly cruel words that were said about my weight, my looks and lack of sexual stamina I hit my breaking point. My wife boarded the plane from Puerto Vallarta heading back to the USA to visit family and Grandkids. She was on the plane, I was on the phone with Salvador. Salvador was an Attorney friend of my soon to be ex-wife. I picked him because I mistakenly thought he could reason with her the unreasonable person that she was and is. I was wrong. No one can reason with a bi polar insane person. But enough said two sides to every story and nothing else needs to be said. I am not here to blame or bash. My only reason for telling the story relates back to chapter one and the Adel story. In her case she was unhappy in my case I was miserable. The breaking point had happen so many time I lost count but finally taking a stand and walking away was the only thing I could do. I am not a violent person and when all reason was gone walking away was my only option. At a certain point in life you realize it is never going to get better.

It was 3 days after my meeting with Salvador my divorce attorney at my home in La Cruz, Mexico, I decided to take a trip and walk around Old Town which was forty-five minutes away from the new house which I had just finished building in a gated community on the Bay of Banderas. As I mentioned it is a stunningly beautiful home which I designed from the ground up every detail was creative and different than others. From the floor to ceiling glass waterfall displaying my huge Swarovski collection. To the built-in notch for more crystal display. Black tile floors, plata Metallica (metallic silver) walls and ceiling stunning in every area. The built-in glass wall in the pool at the Jacuzzis overlooking the ocean. I tell you all that because you now understand how much I wanted out to leave my dream house. If I could walk away from my ten year dream of having a house on the ocean in a gated community I truly must have been miserable.

As I walked around Old Town Puerto Vallarta, I saw maybe the most beautiful human being that I had ever seen. I was on one side of street Olas Altas in Old Town and the beauty was on the other. His features were un-mistakenly European tall I thought over six foot. A face that would make you stop and say WOW dark eyes that haunted me even from a distance. Still knowing he was undoubtedly Mexican but could easily pass for Spanish or Greek.

Starring at each other I noticed he was standing next to massage sign. I am not a massage kind of guy but I thought maybe if he were doing it. So I started to walk to him and half way through the intersection I changed my mind and went left instead of right. So my fleeting though wouldn't go away but I kept walking. Still thinking about him as I walked wondering if our paths would ever cross again and knowing they probably would not. Around the corner a few blocks then I saw the sign for Spartacus an all male gay bathhouse well I guess the, all male is a given, and as casual as I could I quickly darted into the entry. Making my way up the stairs checked in and payed, I got undressed wrapped my large towel around me and started walking around. Came to the theater and sat down a very cute guy came in who I started eyeing and just when I started to make my move another guy came in who totally captured my attention. He looked like a goddess and very familiar but I never could remember faces and still can't. Stopping my move on the first guy and turning my attention to the familiar guy. He was watching me but I could not tell if he was interested or just playing. I caught his eye nodded and then I left the theater went into the dark room. I sat there for what I felt was an eternity but was only about two minutes. I was just about to give up on the beauty and in he walked stood directly in front of me. I reached out my hand he did not stop me, I started rubbing him and then lost all control took him in my waiting mouth and never stopped. We spent the whole time with each other him doing me a I would return the favor several times. We sat and talked for seemed like eternity. I said that I needed to get going was getting hungry. And asked him if he would be interested in having dinner with me. He accepted my invitation to dinner and the conversation continued. I offered to take him to his place but he said ok but just to drop him near by and I could not come to his place. Later I would find out why. So I did and as he instructed and dropped him near the corner where I had turned left earlier. He started to close the door I said "hey I would you like to see you again tomorrow." Without a seconds of hesitation, He said "pick me up here at 11am." Closed the door and left. No phone number nothing else how would I know if he would be there or not? Was I going to drive forty five minutes and find an empty corner? I thought we had a great connection unlike anyone that I had ever met but maybe he was a good actor and was just a kind person to an older over fifty fat guy. A guy according to my now ex no one finds attractive. She said I could never get anyone else and that I was lucky she even stayed with me.

So my dreams were all about him, tossing and turning all night long thinking of him and could not stop. I got up early as I always do awaiting going back to Old Town and wondering if he would actually be there. At 11am I pulled in a dead-end street looked around and didn't see him just as I was going to leave the door to the FJ Cruiser opened and in he came. We drove around trying to decide what to do. I said I needed to feed the dogs again at some point a little later. He said well we can go there and hang out and then come back to town later. I thought that sounded like a good idea and remembered what about lunch he said make me something at your house.

So I started driving and we started talking we never stopped talking about everything under the sun, I poured out my soul about my pending divorce how much I was hurt by her and everything else that two people talk about upon first meeting. Well so I thought. We walked in the house and he seemed mesmerized walked over to the Swarovski waterfall and proceeded to touch one of my favorite and most expensive pieces and as if on cue he broke it. Anyone else I would have escorted them out of the house. Not him I set down the piece and said it could be fixed. To this day it is still broken.

I made us lunch and we went to the pool. He said I don't have a suite and with great laughter I said none of mine will fit you but since the back yard only has an ocean behind us and no one lived next door don't wear one. So we both got in without a suit. Relaxing we swam played slapped the water and he grabbed me turned me around, and then for the very first time in my life I kissed a man. The emotions were overwhelming everything was turned upside down and inside out. Never had I enjoyed anything more. We orally satisfied each other several times hours passed which seemed like seconds, working up an appetite, now was time to make dinner and I did. We held each other orally shared our bodies again and again. I asked him to spend the night and he said he had to teach in the morning I suggested that I would take him home early enough to get ready for his teaching class.

And that's what we did the next morning waking up overlooking the ocean I knew exactly what Love felt like for the first time in my life. I must admit I inadvertently said I Love you on our first dinner but it was said in passing not as a real statement. But this was different there was a deep feeling like I found something for the first time in my life fifty eight years old and finally I felt something so strong there was a physical pain associated with it. A longing that if my heart was full for the first time and I wanted to share everything.

Trying to get it all out in a short amount of time letting go and not caring about the consequences. I was smiling for no reason. I was laughing making everything finally good in my life. I didn't think one second about the negative in my life totally forgot it and just me be me. Finally Free, finally in Love. And yes thinking is it possible to find true love in a fuck place a bathhouse for god sakes. I guess time will tell but who cares. Many people who know me and telling them of our first meeting there was my made up story about hiring him to be my Spanish teacher and we met at Starbucks. That story seemed like an easy sell verse we met in a fuck place and it was a place I knew all too well. The bathhouse story seemed to be less romantic and the coffee shop, teacher story was easier to tell the lie than face the truth.

So I waited around town for him to finish his class. And off we went back to the house where we spent the next few weeks getting to know each other. I told him my deepest darkness secrets more than I had ever told anyone before. He was the first person that I felt comfortable being myself. We laughed like school kids. Played like horny rabbits. Almost daily we would go to Puerto Vallarta so he could do the class'. I could feel myself falling for a guy not in the Anonymous way but real love. I have to confess not once in my two marriages did I ever feel like that. Both marriages I felt I was rescuing someone I married to help them not because I loved them. But until you find and know love how can you compare it? It is not possible you think you know what love is but not really sure always self-doubt. This was real where I could not sleep staring at him for hours while he slept. (For the x-rated continuation of our escapades please read the Story XXX2 in the next section. The details of our affair are in full glory there.) A month went by like it was a day time did not stand still it was on warp speed and each day together was better than the day before. I never wanted this feeling to stop I had found love for the first time in my life. We would go to the nightclub getting in some nights after four in the morning. And get up and do it again the next day. One night on the way home from the clubs in Old Town there was a road block and they were checking for drunk drivers. And I defiantly qualified he was sound asleep and upon getting in the long line I woke him up and said help me I was going to Mexican jail for drinking and driving. He sat up the seat as we approached the police, rolling down the window the police said good evening, I was sober now! I said good evening, he asked how many cerveza have you had and with out lying I said none I don't drink beer and with that he motioned us through and on our drunken way. As I was putting up the window my partner in crime next to me yelled "no beer but fourteen gin and tonics" at that point I was going to kill him. Kept on driving looking through my rearview mirror thinking omg any second they will follow me and pull me over. But we made it home and he is still alive not sure how or why. At that moment I knew there was nothing that would stop us from being together forever so I thought.

As time got closer and closer to her returning I called her and basically said I can not do it any more. And that I had hired and attorney to file the divorce in Mexico, and we needed to get a divorce as soon as possible, she said "there is no fucking way you will ever divorce me." And then total misery was filling my life a wife I was growing to hate and despise. Her attitude toward me was unbelievable her hate grew day by day. She got back and I tried to reason with her but her defiance only grew. Her attitude turned into threats and for the first time in my life I was scarred of what she would do when I was not looking. I would sleep in a different bedroom but locked the door and pulled a night stand in front of the door just incase she would come in a try to kill me during the middle of the night. Even now if feel bad telling this about her but telling the truth means telling the parts that I am not proud of about me and the truth about others. I finally had enough and rented an apartment in Old Town, just down the block from the love of my life. A one block walk to the beach and short Funicular ride to our favorite bar Signature Lounge on the bottom of one of the exclusive condo buildings that over looked all of Puerto Vallarta.

The accusation and fighting begun to truly takes its toll on me. She thought I had fallen in love with my Spanish teacher which was true but she had no idea the She was a He. As time went on our relationship became even more and more interesting and intense. Interesting in the fact that I truly had fallen madly in love with him in the first two days of being with him. But then the literal devastating news came, he was not very subtle about telling me but he kept getting phone calls which he took in private. At first I did not think much of it sometimes in Spanish mostly in English. We had just finished our forth or fifth session of love making and he rolled off and said I have something to tell you. OK What is it I asked, then the avalanche happened, his words so simple and calm "I am married." "What the hell to a woman", I asked no to a man he said. I said "When were you going to tell me that little bit of information?"

"Now I guess", he said we both laughed and then talked for hours. I told him "I do not want to break up a marriage so I need to walk away" He said "No they were in an open relationship." But to find out that even if open it does not mean that someone wants a true competitor in their relationship. Open Relationship was not a new term to me but it became more of a lifestyle than I ever imagined. There is a whole chapter on this later. So as I personally transition from Straight to Bi To Gay my emotions were running ramped. I was all over the scale from happy to sad not knowing what was happening to me. All in all I felt that I was always Bi and still enjoy a lady from time to time. But after you have had anal sex either as a top or a bottom you are pretty much classified as gay.

After I had decided to get divorced and moved out the relief of not having to hide any more was somehow the most relaxed feeling I have ever had. And once I came out to my soon (not soon enough) ex wife my life even got better for me. I asked her for a meeting and she said yes so I drove out to La Cruz and after a long conversation I finally told her that my teacher was a guy and I was gay. Well to say my ex was shocked would be a lie. She started putting everything together and said she knew that there was something wrong with me. And being a Jehovah Witness they had programs to fix me. I told her I had no desire to be Fixed. I had never been happier and there was nothing I wanted except to be happy for me and for her. We both agreed to stay friends well that lasted about as long as I though it would. I am not sure I was out of the gates when she started texting say everything under the sun about me and what a piece of crap I was and that she never loved me. I actually was happy she said it because some how it was easier for me to think that if she never loved me then I certainly was not loosing anything. And I was not making a mistake by walking away.

The divorce agreement that I offered her she accepted then rejected doing exactly what she said she would not do fight everything over and over again. When people say it's not about the money it is truly only about the money. Love has nothing to do with most relationships no matter what money and personal welfare will always over take our senses and Love will always loose. You now either totally agree or are thinking am I correct or am I totally wrong and Love is all there is. But one day I will eventually will be right. Love is all there is unless there is something else. And that something else maybe lust, money, fame, desires or totally unknown at this point in your life. As humans we evolve and change and todays hot point may not be tomorrow's hot point. Once we realize that it is evolving and changing we will truly be happy. Because what we want now is what we want. It was said **"Happiness is not having what you want but wanting what you have."** Well if we could all achieve that and it were totally true what a wonderful place this world would be. We would be happy and content with our place in life and nothing would ever change. Sounds boring on some days and sounds relaxing and peaceful on others.

Finally after years of back and forth the divorce happened and she could stay in the house till it sells. I forgot one thing I needed to have the balls to force the issue and get her out by selling the house. But because I feel guilty she is still living in the four bedroom ocean house in a gated community and I am Living my life. I had moved to Fort Lauderdale, Wilton Manors area because my married partner wanted to live there as soon as he came to the United States. And currently moved to Knoxville to be near family which is what I truly missed in my life. More on that in a bit.

When someone says it sounds like fun being open and free to explore they need to always look deeper everyone puts on a facade and gay people are no different. The transition is not alway easy or kind to us. But it is life, if you have the desire to try Bi with your partner understand the consequences of not coming back from it.

I have had many great moments in my life and so many that I can not begin to express them all. But having grandchildren is one of the greatest feelings that I have never known. When the first one Tyler was born even though technically I was not his true grandpa I never looked at it any differently. I was and still proud of him with the total of five grandkids three as a step grandpa and two boys that my daughter has. Unfortunately my Ex-wife has asked me to no longer have contact with her side of the grandkids. It hurts me greatly and I think about it constantly. But with her being bi-polar and no longer wanting to set her off I only hope they understand it is not because I don't want to see them I just don't want any more problems. But I miss them immensely I use to send them Christmas cards with money but she went nuts. Saying that I was buying their love and not to contact them again. So that is what I have done not proudly but doing it just the same.

I feel this is one reason why I moved to Knoxville to be close to my biological grandsons. I need and want them in my life and as I get older more so. I tell people that it is because of many medical reasons that I moved but the truth is it is to be near family. They are my true reason now for happiness. And as much as I enjoyed having a partner in my life nothing compares to them. The joy in the little one hugging me when I enter the room or the older one still hug-ging me even though he is almost as tall as I am. There is a feeling that makes life worth every struggle in the past, true joy.

Yes having a sexual partner is still what I want and maybe one day my boy friend will rekindle the passion we once had but for now I am content, happy and fulfilled. I will not spend much time talking about our life together or apart because the chapter is not written and not wanting to miss-lead or being inaccurate. But fun we did have and no matter what happens the memories will live on. Especially funny one when we got home about four in the morning and went to sleep so drunk we could barely find our way home. About a hour later he got up I woke up and he was opening the closest door and I asked what are you doing? He said going pee I jumped up and walked him to the bathroom holding his big male member and guiding him to hit the toilet. The next morning I said you were going to pee in the closet and he had no memory. Still one of the funnies moments in life.

STORY 2: THE FIRST TIME ANAL

– XXX –

As we spent the days getting to know what each other was about he slowly worked on my ass trying to stretch me out so he could enter me for the first time ever. On Wednesday afternoon he said I am going to get it done today.. and true to his word he worked the head of his thick manhood into me. Then slowly a bit more he came after 30 minutes and I said omg that fucking hurt he said I only had the head in. Thirty minutes later he was rock hard and again he penetrated me going in about four inches pounded me but still not going all the way. We rested and I said I am done for the day. No way not till I go balls deep. We kissed and played then without warning he lubed my ass and in one full motion was totally within the depths of my ass he pounded it like nothing ever before. We were both drenched in sweat from the hot male on male love making. He shot a load 8 pluses I felt every one of them filling me a deep feeling of true bliss. I being a virgin wondered where all that cum went. Later that evening I found out when his massive load fell to the floor out of my raw ass. The first three months of our torrid affair we made love an average of five times a day on several occasions he was able to do it eight times. Over five hundred times in three months. Which was about equal to my entire life with two wives spanning thirty five years. I was officially hooked I was gay. If you plan on ever experimenting I will tell you start small and work your way up because sometimes we think poop is big and thick so it will fit. I am here to confess it is totally different coming out than something going in to your anal cavity.

Anal is a bench mark for gay people they define ourselves in two categories Top or Bottom. There are some like me that are ninety nine percent oral. I will now confess that there have been only three people totally that have entered me. You have heard the story of my lover and best friend hundreds of times but the other two one was a married couple two males. He was on the bed ass up and I was standing on the floor. I was fucking the husband literally moving the bed as we fucked. His husband a young attractive man and a great friend saw an opportunity and took it with out hesitation. He lubed up came up behind me and started fingering me which I did not think anything of it. But suddenly his cock was in me and were now in a three way love making session. As I pounded his husband he pounded me he truly enjoyed it and honestly so did I, it was one of my favorite love making times ever. To my amazement when he came inside me he quickly moved to his husbands mouth and got hard and came again just about the time I was finishing unloading in his ass. My friends now live in England and even though we totally disagree politically we as still very good friend. That was the one and only time that he fucked me be it was memorable. And yes the bed somehow mysteriously was moved over four feet.

My lover and I set up a meeting with an older guy that I was not totally into but he told me that he did gummy jobs. So we met without much of an introduction we were in bed and my lover was pounding the hell out of him when he told me to feed him and I did putting my hard cock in his mouth and OMG it was memorable the very first time I had ever gotten a blowjob from a guy with no teeth.

He was so talented and he knew just went to apply pressure and when to stop. There was an instinct that as soon as I was about to blow he let up Edging me over and over. My lover kept saying good isn't he and hell yes he was better than I ever expected. I finally could not take it anymore and said I am going to blow my load my lover said wait one minute so we can cum together. I held out and he said ok I am ready and simultaneously he got two loads pumping him full. I will say my load was huge and my lovers is always huge. And the bottom did not gag or even stop sucking till every drop from my head was drained. Then he slowly licked me totally clean, and totally unaware but the huge cock that was just in his ass was not being sucked clean and dry. Even though we did not do a three way due to timing and my move back to the United States I will never forget how kinky and fun that time was for all three of us.

My third bottom happen recently when I had a sub over and to my total surprise he was well endowed and very hot ass that I was rimming and then I slid into his tight ass and for a few minutes then I had the idea to make him rim me so I pulled out and made him eat my ass. I got so excited and he was so good for some reason it just blurted out of my ass lube me and fuck me. He did as requested it had been three years since I bottomed and could only go in a few inches but it truly brought back memories. I took all I could and I said suck my cock and he pulled out and sucked me hard again. I went right back in his ass and shot a big load pulled out and forced my still hard cock down his throat shooting more cum causing him to gag. Great sub he dresses up for me and does as told never questioning anything that is asked of him. His girlfriend has no idea that he is a bi sub whore that will do anything I want. She is meek and mild normal girl that is perfectly happy not knowing her boyfriends true desires and feelings. He loves being used the more the better.

We are setting up a group to use him this is his request. I am much more vanilla that that but also knowing we all have desires and how important it is to have fulfillment in life. So when the situation calls for it I can be much more chameleon like going with the flow and making sure all desires are met. We will see later how important this is to keep a marriage alive and sexually exciting.

3

MARRIAGE AGAIN AND AGAIN

Many people have asked me after my first marriage why would I get married again. Well that is a question that I have asked my self over and over again. The first marriage we were very young and she came from a very very dysfunctional family. She had seven siblings and a father who barely worked and mostly lived off lies and others. I know that my heart was broken by the way she had to work to help to support everyone else as did most of the kids. It was a terrible situation for anyone to be in and I felt that coming from a fairly normal home and being an only child I could and should help. With parents being from Tennessee they never met a stranger so their hearts were always open. We were poor as a child but my mom and dad never stopped giving.

As a kid I never knew when opening the trailer door what was in store. My dad was a big CB radio guy and would always find people in need and take them in, mostly for a brief time a day or two while they were waiting to move in to there place. Most of the people were going to start work at Caterpillar where my dad worked and he always tried to help. So when it came to picking a mate my background was that of helping. The love received from mom and dad was second to none. They always did their best and at the time not realizing that we were poor. And as for many people you don't miss what you don't know. If people understood they were poor it may totally change their lives. I use to watch very poor children play in the ocean in Puerto Vallarta and they were so damn happy! American kids are never as happy as the poorest Mexican child. As Americans we grow up wanting more because others have it and we want it. Keeping up with the Jones is a real as real can get. The desire to have more is only surpassed by our desire of thinking we deserve everything we want. If we do not understand how much we think having more and more Stuff will make us happy then explain to me why there are so many storage units. Where else do people have so much stuff that they are not using and never will use but can't get rid of all the accumulation. Where can you go through out the world where people pay more per square foot to store stuff they will probably move from house to house location to location and never open. We are so attached to Owning that it envelops our way of thinking. Very much like being married has been part of our way of living for hundreds of years. We get married because that is the thing to do have a life partner that will be with us till death. Who in the hell still believes that, very few people truly feel that it will last for ever. But we still do it when we know that over fifty percent of the time we will be wrong. As I will discuss in later chapter may there is a way to make marriage last forever. If you play the stock market and someone told you that you had a greater than fifty five percent chance that in many years of letting your assets grow and become worth a small fortune you will loose fifty percent in one day. Would you still do the investment? Chances are when it is stated like that you would not do the investment. So why are we so willing to do exactly that when it comes to marriage?

So the first marriage ended when I had an affair with a fifteen year younger lady. She had a sexual appetite that was unsurpassed by just about anyone that I had ever seen. To say Kinky would not do it justice. She seduced me and obviously I gave in over and over, I thought it was love but again it caused my divorce from the mother of my only child but then again when I look back the only thing that can be said about my first wife was that I was much happier without her. But what she did to my daughter was nothing short of being cruel. When I decided to write my story I never wanted to use names or accuse anyone of anything because there is truly two sides. But in this case I will tell a few stories just so everyone can understand how hate can take one over and things are done because of hate that never would a person rationally do without the over whelming desire to punish someone at any cost. My first ex would intentionally lock the screen door thus locking my thirteen year old daughter out of the house and she would be freezing till I could come and pick her up and go to the mall. She would do it over and over just to make sure she could inflict pain. How could anyone hurt an innocent child it was not her fault and she had nothing to do with it but my ex would use her to make me feel bad. Honestly it worked, the guilt of what my daughter had to endure was heart breaking. Till this day over twenty five years later I still think about the cruel way she treated my daughter.

Marriage is one thing, children are something on a different level nothing can ever say true love like the love of a child and the connection a person has to the one that you bring life to. With the responsibility of being a father sometimes I felt like I was a terrible dad but other times especially now in my life she is the greatest thing to ever happen to me. My two grandsons are the extension of everything in my life. These are the important moments the one that takes you away from everything you thought you wanted and needed to what Matters. So even knowing early on that I enjoyed the other side of life sexually will never take away the total joy that a child and grand children have brought to my life. And it is not to say that life can not be totally fulfilling without either, because it can be. It will take a different course but it happens when you are not looking for it. You look into that special persons eyes and it happens. We must stop looking for it and let life guide us to our destiny the more we search the less we find. The old saying of You always find what you are looking for does not always hold true when it comes to love.

And I see guys contently try to hook up for the nightly conquest of another strange piece of ass but in reality that is the world of gay life that some follow. Others take a more establishment life where the only thing different is there is a husband or partner for life instead of a wife. They are totally dedicated to each other and never want anyone else in their life. When I talk about gay I also include lesbians but the one thing that I know is that most lesbians are not into open relationships as many gay men are, so mostly everything I have experience in is male to male. I am sure sometimes it will apply to lesbians but not a common as gay men.

When I got divorced for the first time I will say that I was at fault, I was the cheater, the lier and more I am sure. I was never mean or cruel but I was not faithful. So maybe I deserved everything I got, many would say so.

To say that in knowing that I was bi or gay and getting married for the second time can only be described as totally stupid. I knew what I was, and what I would end up being and again I let my need to help someone overpower my true emotional feelings. Knowing that being bi/gay was going to win out and knowing that eventually someone was going to get hurt it was wrong. And for this I totally apology's to everyone that I hurt along the way of my journey into my final life decision.

My second marriage was the most turbulent she was and still is a bipolar depressive. I came home one day and all the plants were thrown all over the house dirt and crap everywhere. Pictures ripped off the walls and she was sitting there like nothing happened. Understanding that by confronting her would only cause more damage to her, I just started cleaning up the dirt up and down the stairs of the townhouse. She had no concern of cost or her actions. This was a side of her that I tried to protect others from seeing. It took some time but finally came down to the fact that you can not help someone who does not want to be helped. Once we were out on a private yacht on New Years Eve having a great time except for her she sat at a table and never talked to anyone never moved for six hours. Friends would sit with her and try to open a conversation but she just sat there staring into the distance but looking right at them. Everyone was concerned and asked me what drugs she was taking but to my knowledge she never did any drugs. The only reason for saying any of this would be to show how I slowly became totally disinterested in her and nothing she could do would bring me back to loving her. The more of her putdowns and demeaning me left scares that time will never erase. Don't misunderstand this is not why I became Bi or Gay, I think I was always that way. You will see in other chapters we did have fun at swinger clubs and such.

One thing that will be said about all human beings is that they for the most part know the truth. They understand that deep down inside they understand when things are not just right. But due to our desire to be loved we overlook the obvious. When something is right in front of us we act like we don't see a thing. From a layman's point of view the moment you start to question your feelings and trustworthiness of your partner, chances are it is time to walk away. No matter how hard that is, when you just sit and take the lumps you are inflicting more damage to yourself. Because in the end loving someone because you are trying to help them is not love, it is charity. No one deserves you, no one deserves to take your happiness and make it theirs. No one has a need greater than yours put yourself first and everything will fall into line. You can have all the passion in the world for others but if you fail yourself you fail everyone, eventually.

To answer the question why get married if I knew I was gay or at least bi is not easy. I truly do feel that it is more about being accepted because of my job and friends. Job has so much to do with our overall decisions in life but we truly do not give it as much weight as we all should. I was in a position where everyone in the company knew me and I knew more customers than anyone else. We had thousand of customers and I really had worked with most of them directly or indirectly or they had attended my seminars. There was a big desire not to let people and workmates down. So there it was much easier to admit an affair that that I was gay. So the lie continued I was the biggest fool in the world I could have just not married and done my thing on the side but I did not. Everyone loved my new wife and thought she was great because the didn't know the truth and hiding her problems only created more problems. But in totally honesty again damn I hate telling the truth so much when it makes me look so bad but truth is the truth. I built her up as a goddess knowing all well she was crazy. But in blaming me for being stupid I stayed and tried to minimize my mistakes. For years I was unhappy sorry not unhappy, miserable. Daily I wanted it over and daily I stayed, year in and year out, this was no life for even a cheating lying jerk.

If there was one bit of advice that I could pass on it would actually be two, number one always be Kind, and number two take care of yourself first. If you are truly Kind you may not change everyones mind but you will do it with grace and heart. And secondly if you do not put yourself first, you will become or are a totally unhappy person that only looks for the negativity in life. It will start to consume you and sadly the only person that doesn't realize what you have become is you. Because negative people don't think they are negative they look at everyone else and think they are the problem.

I have done a ton of soul searching looking deep inside me and these are the two things that you can change about yourself today. And your environment around you can bring you down to their level so change your environment. Notice I did not say change them, because that is impossible no matter how hard you try it does not happen. Only change that will be made is you changing you, spending time working on someone else is just a waste of time. We honestly think because we changed then we can help someone else that supposedly loves us to change too. Wrong they never love you that much. They may try to change but slowly or quickly they will revert back to what you are trying to escape. So when it comes to real change, Is it easy, no it is not, is it the best for you, yes it is. I can compare this to politics in a very basic way. How hard it is to walk away from a political party that has so changed and that we continually disagree with in our head and heart, but because everyone else stays you stay too. Weather you are a Republican or Democrat it is hard to walk away from everything you thought they stood for and maybe you are wrong because everyone else you know is staying with them. But when you look deeply you find you stay for exactly the same reason. What would others think, how can I justify my actions, everyone thinks I think like that, I am happy with everything and so on and so on it goes. If you want things to change then change them. If you want your situation to change change it. No one will do it for you, no one! There is no savior there is only you!

STORY 3: CLOSE TO HOME

– XXX –

Checking www.sls.com a couple had left me a message about getting together one afternoon. They lived in Rock Island IL just five minutes away from my house. I talked to the wife and after setting it up she wanted me to chat with the husband so after long conversation we set up a time and met at their house. She was a beauty long brown hair tall very thin with voluptuous tits. On the shorter size about five foot three. She had those kind of eyes that would or could make you do anything. Dark and mysterious alway making you wonder what she was thinking. And think she did. He was a big man 6'4" strong muscular the rugged outdoors type. He was a hard working man with calluses on his hands. The typical red neck kind of guy that you would sit at the bar and drink beer. Could just tell he was a sports nut and honestly zero the type that would ever play sexually with a guy.

When I got there we sat and talked 10 minutes she said ok enough talk you two go to the bedroom and get undressed. So he and I went to the bedroom undressed and came out to the living room to find her beautiful body nude with her huge tits and unbelievable nipples standing to attention. She was spread leg and was fingering herself seeing the moisture building up between her legs I wondered if she was a squirter or very moist. We were ordered to sit on each side of her and the instruction were that she and only she would control the sex that was about to commence. We were told to suck her nipples and so we started sucking her tits.

Her husband had never done anything with a man and she told me on the phone, and that she want to turn him bi but I had to say that I never had been with a man also when we met. This was the part of those eyes that we so telling and I knew we were both in for major trouble.

So after a hot time getting us both hard sucking her voluptuous tits, she said do you boys want to fuck me? Yes we do. Ok if you want pussy I want to watch you each suck each others cock. He said "hell no" I put up a very convincing argument and said "no way." She told her husband if he ever wanted to fuck her again he would have to suck cock and get sucked. Both of us still saying no she fingered her pussy and slid her fingers in his mouth. Are you sure babe she said you will miss this the rest of your fucking life. So she told me to go first I said I would but only if he was ok I didn't want any trouble. Finally after a long conversation I was between his legs. I made it a point not to look at his cock while we were playing with her because I did not want him to catch me. He had obviously gone soft because his wife made a comment about how small it was now.

So I got down between his legs and timidly started sucking his limp cock. The more I sucked he started to come to attention and then more attention and finally he was sporting a nine inch thick piece of manhood. She said see babe you love it don't you? And he admitted it was very good. He told her between kisses that I sucked as good as she did as they talked she was all excited fingering her pussy like crazy. She kept him more than occupied kissing and putting tit in his mouth. Then suddenly she stood on the couch and lowered her young hot pussy to this mouth. He was making her moan so loud I thought the house next door could hear her. Then all of a sudden she stood and said ok change positions. To say he was reluctant would be an under statement. After some real coaxing and sexual persuasion from his beautiful bombshell wife, he went down on my rock hard cock. He was so timid it was almost cute he was awful at sucking but he did it. And as I was thinking it over I was much more experienced and I think he knew it was not my first time. She was licking his balls while he was sucking me and that position was perfect timing. She could not see him but I said to him lets turn the tables and do her. And then we both said ok bitch now your turn.

I got up and started eating her pussy while he stood and shoved his cock down her throat. Asking if it was ok to slide my cock in her he said "don't ask just fuck her good." And we took several times fucking her and when one was fucking the other had his cock in her mouth. Every time she tired to talk we shoved a cock in her mouth. Over and over again we exchanged position. I almost came at least four times but holding back like never before. Back and forth for 30 minutes she came over and over again. She was so happy carrying on like it was Christmas morning and she just got a new car. She broke out in a sweat and said it was the hottest fucking ever. We relaxed caught our breath and she slowly got on her knees and began licking us both off. She got up after sucking his cock hard and kissed me shoving all of his juice in my mouth. And said swallow it, I did gag but I did as requested. She fingerer her hot pussy got every drop of her own juices shoved them in my mouth and said lick. He really started to get hard again, got up and shoved his huge member in her mouth said to me thanks but now you can leave this will be our time. I quickly gathered up my belongings and left without bothering them in thrill of the moment of passion. Feeling grateful just being allowed to experience it one time. He called and said he loved it but just couldn't do it again mentally. Thus ending their experiment in the bi lifestyle. But in the back of my mind somewhere I know she has convinced him to do it again. She is the type person who did not take no for an answer.

4

THE LIES "WHO WAS I PROTECTING"

When I sat down to write this book there was an honest doubt if I could be totally honest in every facet of my life. Outwardly I thought I would be protection my daughter, grandkids and ex wives but the reality is I would only be protection myself. By not being open then why do it, why tell some if I could not tell all. So with every attempt to be transparent, something politicians say when we all know they are lying, so that may not be the best word. But you get my meaning I am going to tell and have told everything, leaving nothing too interruption and conspiracy theory. But that was not always the case for years I hid who or what I was and the lies someday were overwhelming.

There were times in my life where my wives would really want to play and fuck around, other times they wanted to make love to me and many and I do mean many of those times I have already sucked several cocks and got a couple blow jobs there was nothing left for them. Time after time I would run off and have sex with someone or several someones. I would make up every excuse in the book and over and over again it was me I was totally was sexed out. When my lies started they never ended and amazingly I never got caught they would just right it off as he works hard and is exhausted. Thank goodness I was a very hard worker so I got away with it most of the time. There were a few times where they did not take no and I would have to use all my very substantial oral skills to satisfy them without them knowing that I was not able to get hard. I remember one time that I actually was down there eating away and she said fuck me and I said sorry I got so hot eating you I came so I had to let out a bit of pee to have a wet spot so she believed me. So then the lies compounded when I would say "you got me so hot I could not hold it back and I just shot with out knowing" they would think damn I still turn him on. When the answer was just the opposite. Others turned me on, Anonymous turned me on, not the same old same old.

But when it comes down to who, or maybe the better word is what are you protecting, I can say it was other people, as I said family, wives, etc that was Bull Shit. Most guys do what they do LIE, because they are protection their money. They want to get away with it so they don't go through a divorce. We are mostly cowards when it comes to losing our money so we stay in a situation that are lies and cover ups. Let me say after two divorces they are expensive. When my first wife finally had had enough and Asked her what she wanted for her birthday present and she said "a Divorce", I though to myself "damn I wasn't willing to spend that much."

It is true when we say it's not about the money it is all about the money. It is said that a majority of marriages fail over money, BS they last longer because of money if it were not for money they would have ended a long time ago. And honestly after talking to many people in my life, friends, business customers etc many and I mean many would get divorced if they were not going to loose half of what they have. So they hang in there and go through the motions of nothingness.

The protection question is alway one of our first thoughts it should be about family but its not about family but money. So now we understand its about money then that makes it easier for guys and gals to cheat. They have a crap marriage and they are only staying there because of the money so it becomes less connective to the emotional ties of family. This in the back of your mind, making it even easier to cheat and cheat more. No one in their right mind would say I Love Money more than Family but who said we are in our right minds. But the moral disconnect of family and dollars are truly deep in our thoughts and it helps justify the life style that we have chosen.

I recently reconnected with an old friend she had it all the million dollar house, retired with more money than they could ever spend but had not had sex in years with anyone including her husband. And in our conversation after her husband had died she admitted finally she only stayed in a sexless marriage because of the money. She could not walk away from the constant bombardment of gifts and having anything she wanted at her fingertips was more valuable to her than the passion she truly desired. The biggest difference is that she did not stray not once, even though there was a point that if the opportunity presented itself I think she would have. There was even a time that I thought she and I may have an affair. But that fleeting thought soon evaporated.

It's not all the time are we all prone to cheating, or even looking for it but give the right situation we could all be persuaded. I remember being infatuated with a coworker she was so hot and available. One night where a group of us were out after work on Friday night she got a bit drunk and I being the gentleman that I truly am said let me drive you home and finally she agreed. Got to her house and I said good night she said walk me in, I agreed and asked if I wanted a beer I reminded her I did not drink beer so she said nothing sat down next to me lay back and lifted up her skirt lifted her leg and slowly poured beer slowly trickling down her leg and told me I bet you will drink this beer, lick it off she said and I obliged just as the beer got to where her panties use to be I imagined, she stopped me and said ok now you drink beer go home to your wife. Truly my first real cock tease!

I got home and my wife said you smell like beer and I laughed yea they dared me to drink one but I only got the first sip and spit it out on myself. Another lie but a fight everted. And the bank account was still in tacked. Many people will read this and think what a cold bastard, and maybe that is a better way of looking at it, because the truth in their life may be too much to handle. That is the real reality many of us are just as much in denial about our lives as our partners are about lying about their real life behind the walls and bank accounts.

Don't get me wrong yes we all love our family and never want to see them hurt in any way. But when we are in the decision making process in the back of our mind we have an agenda and it is not always what we say it is out loud.

So Who was I protecting, may have been better worded What was I protecting? Now we know the answer it was not personal it was financial but in the long run it still cost me, both.

STORY 4: KNOXVILLE PORN ARCADE

– XXX –

While visiting family in Knoxville Tennessee I stopped by the local arcade many times. Small but horny guys. There are only 8 booths and a 15x10 room that was fun to stand in the dark and get some group action going. With 4-5 guys bending over and sucking each other, Very hot. One evening I stopped by and went to the back booth and a husband and wife were in there with the door open so I stood in the booth across from them she motioned me over. They were much older couple than I normally liked but she was very intriguing looking older but classy in a slutty way. Short brown hair showing off her perfect shoulders with a sweater pulled down over the shoulders. Went in the booth she closed the door. Up close I got a much better look she was exquisite looking much more beautiful that first thought. She had what could be described as a classic movie star look from the fifties only with short hair.

Quickly she pulled up her sweater to expose her huge tits that were totally hidden by the bulky sweater. They were a D Cup with huge nipples and aureolas. She told her husband to sit down and she grabbed me I started sucked those big titties getting her hot and wet. Then without warning she looked at her hubby and said that he was mine to use and degrade. Her husband was normal even plain looking and she was totally out of his league. I would guess he was a business executive that enjoyed being the blunt of humiliation due to a high pressure job. This is very common in the alternative life style. I am not that guy normally that like abuse but I felt this was their thing so I would join in their fantasy. I was fingering her then choking him putting all my fingers in his mouth that just came out of her extremely wet and hot pussy, she liked that. He would get all the juice off and over and over gaging him. Then she pulled out my hard cock and made him suck it. And she asked me, no told me to slide my cock into her pussy and to his mouth back and forth. And just to see how far I could take it I rubbed my cock head in her poop hole and made him lick it off over and over. Then sucking her tits turning her around and fucking her. All of a sudden with out warning I shot my load. Pumping her full. I quickly apologized to her saying it just happened. She said shut up that's what I wanted and that she had been squeezing me so hard to make me cum.

She made him beg for the cum inside her pussy. He sat on the floor with her straddling him and she released my huge cum load directly into his mouth. Then I made him clean me up licking my cock and balls. We both decided to take a break but she knew he needed more humiliation so even though he resisted we stripped him and made him knell in the dark room and she and I were kissing and when a guy would walk in the room I would lift up her sweater and fondle her huge tits. We would tell the guys to feed him their cock and cum. Finally she whispered in my ear he doesn't ever want to eat ass. Well of course we brought him a very tall, young, hot tight ass guy with a big cock. Her hubby looked at the guy with puppy dog eyes and the youngster took out his massive cock. OMG I wanted that cock but I played my part he started sucking his massive member then she whispered and told the young guy to turn around we forced her hubby's head against the wall and ass in his face we forced him to eat it till he could barely breath we both think he started liking it. Not sure if it was the young hot ass or if he just fell in love with ass eating but he became a pro. He did so well the guy said omg I am cumming we quickly turned around and shoot the load in his mouth. He gagged but the cum just kept flowing. And now according to his wife ass eating has become his favorite thing to do. I have chatted with her many times but never met again, every time I stop by the arcade always hoping to run into them but never have. I am always amazed how many ladies love to watch their man get fucked, suck cock, get sucked, eat ass and fuck guys. Very impressed by the open minds some couples have. And the willingness of men to share their wife and wives to share their husbands. As we will talk later about this may be the difference in a great relationship and divorce. Each person getting what they want and need.

5

DO YOU REALLY WANT TO KNOW?

One of the largest questions concerning what you have learned so far is if your partner, husband, wife or other had a secret life would you want to know? And the bigger question would be what would you do about it? *When you start to wonder about your overall relationship what does it come down to? If you find out could you bring yourself to the understanding and live with the truth no matter what? Would you consider joining the lifestyle if you find out there is an alternative hidden lifestyle? And if you conclude that you can't deal with the situation, are you willing to give up the life you now know? Is your moral compass so strong that there is no way you would consider staying or living the new life?*

I will tell you right now they will NOT stop living the lifestyle they have been accustomed to living. Maybe they can stop for a while but once it is in your DNA you can't stop longterm. Remember also, this is not Love for them in most cases, it is only a sexual fantasy that they have repressed for years or covered up for years. And now for what ever reason they are acting on it and or they have always acted on it, but now you are just starting questioning. The questioning comes in two forms internally you ask yourself or directly you ask them.

The desire for anonymous is not going to change just because you had a heart to heart talk and they feel sorry. We do feel sorry but we will not change please understand that. Maybe there is a chance a very very small percent would change but please make every decision you make based on your partner NOT changing. Because there is no way you can actually think you are the very very small percentage where your partner feels so bad he or she changes. And the fact that you think I am wrong is going to cause the situation to continue without you figuring it out. We are very good at deception and lying so now that your partner knows you are never going to accept it the lies will only become more underground and more deceptive. They will start to check in more and sending photos etc only to confirm they are where they say they are. All of this is to mask what they are truly doing. Let's get back to the question that you have to consider knowing they are not changing.

Look at each question with the facts they are still going to do what they do either in the open or behind your back. There alway is a seedy dark room or a high end hotel room, a random pickup spot or an anonymous hole through the wall, for them to find to fulfill their desires.

Is your moral compass so strong that there is no way you would consider having a partner with this kind of desires? For some, the total discussion stops here. There is no way to live with someone who has an issue of this type. You will never ever consider living this life based on religions or moral values that you have now and or have been brought up with your entire life.

Nothing they can do or say will change your mind. And to you I say good for you! You have taken a stand and not going to budge no matter what happens to your family. No matter how hard it is financially. No matter what happens to the kids, this is your stand, equally as strong as what you have learned your partners stand will be. That they will not change, either can you. There it is, you would want them to be different and not the way they are, but they can't, remember either can you! I will not or can not judge from either side of the situation, because we all need to understand and accept that there are deep needs desires and reasons why we feel how we feel.

If you can't deal with the situation, are you willing to give up the life you now know? Will you look back and say you made a mistake soon or long after it is over? One other fact that will not go unnoticed the person who has the altered life will miss everything just as much as you. But somehow you will think that they are having the time of their life and they are the cause of your misery. You make the life you choose, and since you have a choice, and if not living or being with the person any longer is your choice, so if its your choice, at least Choose to be HAPPY. And when it comes to thinking about the other person the Anonymous the trouble maker so to speak. Their life is not all fun and games maybe for a short while it is but long term they are nothing more than a regular person just trying to get through life day to day. And speaking from experience the grass is not always greener or abundant as you would think.

Don't let anyone define you! Both of you will have to come to the realization that this is maybe the most defining moment of your life. Separation or divorce is much harder than getting married. We all have mostly happy memories of marriage but few people have happy memories of divorce. So when all the questions arise from above are you willing to give it up? If they have been doing it for years with out your knowledge what would be different? There it is again Now you know and knowing is not always the same as wanting to know. We think we want to know but once we find out do we wish we did not know. My mother always said "there will always be a Santa as long as you believe". So can that translate to this situation, you may know the truth without knowing. We are all in some way or another material beings and as much as we don't want to think that having what we have is extremely important to us, it is. Giving up part of what we have in materials is and always will be a consideration to every outcome. The decision is yours and only yours because the truth is, you can not do what is best for everyone else, only what is best for you. And once your choice or mutual choice has been made do yourself a favor let it go. You can spend the rest of your life bitter and mad but that truly helps no-one. You will undoubtedly take it out on the kids, your friends, family etc. And before you know it you are the person they all hate, run from, disown. The old saying misery loves company well once you go down the road with misery you will only surround yourself with those kind of people because all the good people can't stand being around you anymore. And then your misery takes the next tole on everything you touch and you will never get out of the rollercoaster ride of constantly becoming the victim. Then years pass and you still have not found anyone because you let someone else's action define you. Standup for yourself, but fucking standup don't standup by blaming move to your better place and make your life better. Do what you need for you and your family.

When you start to wonder about your overall relationship what does it come down to? As just stated what is best for you is the important factor. Besides the material items in life there is real life relationships to consider. If knowing changes everything in your relationship and it will, sometimes in a positive way and sometimes not. Can you ever be intimate again knowing? Can you have passion for someone that you love or use to love? When you are intimate can you get past your current knowledge of what is going on without you? I am sure a physiatrist could and have written entire books just on this topic. It will not be easy no matter what you decide. But one thing for sure you will not be able to fake it long term you may decide you will try and go through the motions. No one wants to live just going through the motions people want love, passion, sex, fun and excitement and going through the motions destroys all of that.

Expanding your mind and feeling far beyond what you thought ever possible. How in one day can you make a decision that for maybe years and years you thought life was one way, only to find out that none of what you thought was real. That everything was tainted, was it ever real? Were you deceived from the start? Were you in a relationship at all? And when it comes down to it you have to only go by feeling. If you felt in love you were. If you felt you had a great relationship you did. Nothing that you felt can change now, looking forward yes it will change but looking backward take it for what it was, your feelings. Because what is true love but only a feeling. Once you start looking back and thinking nothing was as it seemed then you only make what's to come, harder. The resentment will grow and you will never have a fond memory, ever. So this is the most important thing I will say in the entire book, "DON'T GIVE UP YOUR PAST TO CREATE YOUR FUTURE."

It happened let your past happiness live and the memories become true because they were. The future is totally unknown in your situation but the fact is, that is true for every person in the world. So let your future have as much of a chance to be great as you allowed your past. Yes it is true most of us seem to change our past to fit the narrative that we thought it should be not what it really was. So many times our past is much better or much worse that the reality. So in truth being our guideline is your life better or worse than you remember. One thing that is guaranteed it is not exactly what you remember. So in knowing that our past is not true what is going to happen to our future? Are we finally going to take off our rose colored glasses and see it for what it really is? Or are we going to take off our grey glasses and see it for what it really is? Because depending on our situation we will pick one pair. Only you can take off the glasses and say enough is enough I am going to live my truth life.

I am not going to blame others for my failures and know that only person to blame is me, no matter what. If something goes wrong now in our society we look for the someone to blame without thinking maybe it is us. Our future is the same as it always was it could take a long time to see that but we make our future no one else can define us or create us it is up to us!

Would you consider joining? If you are considering staying are you considering joining in the new lifestyle your partner has chosen? The question of total changing life as you know it is as real as it gets. Maybe a small percentage are totally relieved when you find out the truth, because you also have had the desire and never acted or you have acted and your secret is deeper and some say darker because you have not or will not confess. If you join, it is certain because you have had desires unspoken in the past.

This revelation may open up a side of both of you that will unleash the greatest passion ever in your relationship. As you have or will read in the XXX stories many ladies love the control sex has in their life. And what a better way to control your mate than you letting or making them live out his or her sexual prowess in front of you and you calling the shots. That is one way that people accept the new lifestyle. With almost every couple I have ever met or been with the husband or male partner lets the lady control what happens. This is understandable because they want to keep them happy and when they make the call there are many less problems. And in total honesty it is the way the guy gets to do more because even if she does not tell him what to do many things just happen naturally during the sex. Another way is that you do it together and mutual enjoyment for each with the other, and if not joining in at least being in the same room or area so your voyeuristic side is on display. Totally knowing what is going on and doing your own thing at the same time or just being around will make it easier to handle because there is no longer a hidden agenda or life.

Some of the strongest marriages I have ever known are in the or an alternative lifestyle. They are so connected no jealousy none, they are free and both know what is going on and their only goal is for their partner to be totally happy and satisfied. And when one is that happy they only can bring total joy and happiness to the relationship. As you will read about in the XXX Bi-Club Parties the couples are best friends and lovers and both in a totally satisfied situation. As many of the parties that I attended in my life not one time did anyone have a bad word to say about the other one. They understood that there was limited time and they totally made the best of every moment. It is one of the relationship situations where we seldom tell everything about our thoughts and lives but all is on display for the partner to see and join. We all hide something and many times it is so basic no reason not to tell it but we just don't. This is the side of our personality where we would never consider being one hundred percent open. And I am not saying that open couples tell everything because it is not true. But when it comes to the biggest part of their life they are more open than most couples.

One of the biggest reasons the one partner does not know

about the other, is they think their partner is telling all. And they just have no time to do anything with their busy schedule. With our busy life it would never occur that it would even ever happen, so it never even crosses their mind that anything could ever happen. Many people when they find out one thing that almost always comes up is when did they have time to do anything? There is always time. The old saying if there is a "will there is a way", could never be more true. Give you an example I was visiting my stock broker and they were moving to another floor of the same building. He was so proud of it so he took me up there and no work was going on but we did start working on each other. We were very careful but for a few minutes we were totally exposed to anyone that happen to walk in. At that point we got nervous and decided not a good idea to continue so I just waited a week till he could meet me at my house. We made up for the missed time and finished what we started. So when you think there is no time there is.

I have filled you with more questions than answers which is always the case. But now if you never though about your partner cheating with an Anonymous you are thinking about it now. And before you start inquiring about your concerns start answering the questions now, so you don't go into it blind sided. I will say from past history going in blind is not the situation you want to be confronted with again do it on your terms. Let the other person be the one back on their heels for a change. Have your answers and question ready and answered. It will make your life better giving you the chance for preparation.

In preparation I will give you a few tips through out the book. And here are just a few

1. Start setting money aside each week set money aside for you and your family. Call it your vacation fund that way there is a reason if you are wrong about your concerns.
2. Will, make sure your Will is up to date. Make sure everything is stated and you can make it iron clad where you can benefit no matter what if legal in your state.
3. Even if you have a Prenuptial Agreement change it to include a morals clause that if they cheat on you it is null and void.
4. Life insurance make sure you or at least the children are always covered.
5. Investments make sure all investments are put in both names and need both to make changes.
6. Pensions make sure the same is done, where you are on the pension and as part of the prenuptial you will get fifty percent if there is a delusion of the marriage.
7. Car Title make sure you each have your names on your own car just a tip pick the one with no loan.
8. House Title must be done with both names using the word "And" not the word "Or".
9. Name on Credit cards make sure you have your own credit card with out your partners name on it. Just another tip use the credit card with partners name for all purchases so the balance is in their name.

Remember these are good ideas for anything and if you are wrong about your concerns and what to do about them you will have many things covered for life ahead anyway.

STORY 5: WASHINGTON D.C. THEATER

− XXX −

When I was at a Chef convention in Washington D.C. I was able to find an adult entertainment theater. Not like anyplace I had ever seen. Huge vaudeville type theater with male strippers dancing up and down the isles. Behind the screen was a maze of booths, dark halls, pyramid of beds and more. Directly behind the screen was a locker room. Then leading to a dark hall totally blacked out narrow oneway hallway. Leading out to a very large square semi dark room. More rows of booths and ending up with a pyramid of beds 4 levels high. Looked like mostly men were going in the dark area while there were a few ladies watching their husbands suck off guys in the theater.

So I made my way through the dark hallway and everywhere I touched there was a cock or ass in the dark. With little alcoves it was about 40 feet of total darkness. It was exciting finding a truly anonymous cock or mouth around every corner or indention. As I walked through I stopped and sucked two and filled one mouth with my cock. I only spent about ten minutes in the dark maze but very erotic. Then walking into the semi dark large room where several groups of men were allowing everyone to use them as they wanted. The guys were so inviting as I walked by they would pull me into their group some handing me their cock to suck I got down on my knees and was sucking a beautiful mans large cock he invited several others to join us, at one time I was servicing four cocks. Not truly being able to see the guys more feel them was very exciting. But true to form I always smelt them and touched them and smelled my hand to make sure it was clean. Not really worrying about the true issue of STD's. Moving from one to another each one was a twenty something back then I was late thirties. After exhausting my jaw I took a break and finally needing to rest I adventured on into the extremely small glory hole booths area, they left the doors open so everyone could watch, two guys on each side with cocks through and a guy with cock through the only closed door. Three cocks at a time had no idea how the guy in the closed booth was keeping them all happy but he was. With the proximity being so close to Washington DC, I always wondered how many politicians were there getting their release anyway they could. Once done fucking the public they would show up and fuck or get fucked anonymously over and over.

The next area was a three level pyramid of beds stack high in a stair step affect. All three levels had guys on them it was hard to see the top but easy to see two guys tag teaming another guy and from the sound of it the two guys were big in all the right areas. But below them on each bed were several couples making beautiful love to each other it was very, very erotic to watch. These guys put all lovemaking on public display.

As I was leaving I noticed in the back of the theater there were steps where the orchestra use to play. It was not well marked and I was not even sure that I should venture up there but, you know by now I am always up for and adventure. The stairs lead to an entirely new adventure reaching the top. There was a lot of blowing going on just not a French horn. Guys bent over a table asses up and ready for any anonymous cock or tongue. Over and over non stop they would take load after load. One guy had his wife bent over big ass exposed telling guys to do whatever they wanted to her. I watched in total amazement as a huge black mountain man would fuck a guy on the table pulled out his massive tool and into the ass of the guys wife. Then like rehearsed the husband got on the table his wife jumped on his cock and the big black cock went in her ass again. She was getting double teamed and what a pounding she was getting.

This went on for an extremely long time, occasionally a guy from the other table would pull out his cock and the couple would orally share him while she already had her hubby in the pussy and the black cock in her ass. When the black guy said that he was ready to finally shoot they ask for him to bring the cock to there face so they could share the load. He graciously obliged shot the biggest load as they feasted on his pure white thick milky load. Another guy started pumping her pussy joining the husband's cock inside the pink heaven. They didn't take a break when I walked away they seemed like they were just getting started. No idea how both cocks fit in her pussy but defiantly not her first time.

I quickly figuring out this is where the couples go in the theater , I am a slow learner.

Then the experience started over, one lady was sitting on a large couch with her husband standing next to her. She was unbuttoning her blouse. He saw me looking and motioned for me to come over I said hello as I was talking to him, his wife unzipped my pants and took my cock in her mouth. I reached down grabbed a hand full of her big tits. She looked up and said you want some he said yes and went to his knees they shared me kissing sliding down both sides of my erect penis. She then asked if I would eat her pussy "hell yes". He stood stroking his cock while I was down eating her out, I looked up what the hell it was huge, he saw my eye on him so I raised up and took him in my mouth. Working him over he said lets fuck her she got on her knees and we took turns with her, a group gathered she was sucking several guys over the back of the couch. He unloaded in her hot pussy, and for the first time I unloaded in a pussy that had already been filled with a huge hot thick load. It felt so different that anything I ever felt. It was like my cock enveloped in a thick jell. I blew my load and as soon as I pulled out she turned over and said it's all yours baby. He went down and sucked every drop of thick cum out of her pussy. It was amazing to see a guy that loved cum so much. Two of the guys she was sucking said they were ready to blow and she said go ahead hunny take the loads they both shot in his waiting mouth and they kissed snowballing the loads. Damn sex is exhausting got in my rental car and drove back to the Sheraton and slept like a baby.

6

THE SIGNS/WHAT TO LOOK FOR

This is a chapter that will or may give up secrets of how to tell if your partner is cheating not only with an Anonymous but others. There are tell tail signs that this chapter uncovers, it's the what to look for, if you suspect or even if you don't.

And I am not sure how many of these you will recognize but chances are you have noticed many but thought nothing of it. And in some cases you can have dozens of these signs and nothing is up at all. So please don't jump to conclusions but when you start to look you will see a pattern and that pattern will lead you to the final conclusion that you need to have the talk of talks. Or there is a chance you saw the signs and choose to ignore it because you do not want to know the truth? This is the age old question "would you be better off not knowing", that we hit upon in the previous chapter.

THE SIGNS

1. Starting to change hours of work without notice
2. A smell of different cologne
3. Changing cologne brand

4. To tired for sex
5. Going for a drink after work with the guys
6. Going to watch a game at the bar
7. Calling the office and not there
8. Weekend boys trips
9. Changing password on devices
10. Asking if you want to go on a trip and visit family, college friends etc with out them because they are too busy
11. Having a Change of cloths in car
12. Golf game last a lot longer than normal
13. You may hear, I was talking to _____? and the time got away
14. While you were away neighbors saying "he was gone a lot working hard"
15. Spending more time away from home in hotels for work
16. Not attending as many children's events
17. Making unusual looks at same sex or opposite sex
18. Nodding to perfect strangers
19. Running into a work mate that you never heard of
20. Listening to different music
21. Making comments I want to stay current
22. Change in dress
23. Starting to get in better physical shape
24. Increased gas usage
25. Hiding text messages
26. Not coming to bed as usual
27. Closing compter or phone abruptly
28. Talking more about opposite sex
29. Watching eyes scan parking lot of porn place
30. Interest in walking trails at parks
31. Faking sickness

32. Red çock with a excuse I jacked off in the shower
33. Scratches, bit marks, bruising, etc
34. Looking at cookies and there is no search history
35. A change in attitude about gay people
36. Deodorant and or cologne in the car
37. Running errands that take longer
38. Less interest in sex overall
39. Looking at phone with a higher degree of frequency
40. Reading text or phone and smiling
41. Looking at you making sure you were not watching
42. Calling out to find out where you are in the house
43. Moving office around
44. Changing where they normally sit
45. Setting up new email accounts
46. Finding a second phone
47. Different hair cut
48. Mannerisms change
49. Condom, lube etc. found in places different than normal
50. Carrying more cash than normal
51. Not using credit cards as much
52. More distant in thought
53. If you ever hear a conversation that makes no since it could be code.
54. Asking more about your friends
55. Shower as soon as they get home saying rough day need to relax be right back
56. Throw clothing directly into the washing machine and many time putting the detergent in and starting it up.
57. Mentioning the person over and over from work

58. Them saying "you know the married guy" makes it sound more innocent
59. Spending time at the gym
60. While at the gym spending lot of time in steam rooms

Not one of these or even several of these signs is a red flag but when many of them are put together and all about the same time means there maybe an issue again nothing defined. Many of the signals are signs that they may have an ongoing lover and the others more of an anonymous lovers. Remember many times to hide the acts the person changes in a more positive way. This is done to cover up the guilt and remorse they have about what is going on in their real life. What many people see is the made up life and the True life/Real life is what happens in the shadows.

Once a person is involved in this life you may never find out unless they confess. And most of them will deny, deny, deny and never confess even if you caught them with a cock in their mouth. This is the nature of the cover up if they deny long enough it will become true. We all have stories that we have told for so many years that they are now true to us, even though the first time we told it was a lie but over time we come to believe our own lies.

The next big lie will be if caught that was the only time and they were experimenting just to see if it could help your sex life. LIE first of all they have been doing it for years and just now got caught and second of all they don't care about improving your sex life they care about improving their sex life.

There is nobody that wants to live on the edge and wonder about their partner but if you are truly worried you may have a reason to be. Normally we have a built in instinct that something is going on but due to our love for our partner we over look the signs and let it go. The signs will be there not one person I know of can get away with it unless their partner either doesn't care or is totally oblivious to the situation. And the thinking of it could never happen to me is the perfect situation when it can or has happened. I hate to sound so pessimistic but remember this is a book about honesty and what people say or do when they think know one is watching is the true person.

I remember running into a work mate in a porn cinema/arcade and without thinking I said hey Mike how are you? Just then remembered where we were. At the annual Christmas party he never got close and never let his wife get near me and before the encounter we would sit at the same table. And somehow from that day forward I never talked to him again in the office even though we use to chat weekly. It's not only the partner that is kept in the dark but all family, friends and work mates. So keeping up the hidden truth is much harder than having a simple affair. An affair most guys tell their best friend if its the opposite sex but not if it has to do with same sex. I remember having an affair with a girl that work indirectly in the company as an outside product representative. My friends knew I was playing with her but they did not know that I had a secret life far beyond her. And that many times a side playmate/affair is a cover up to what is really going on. This is true in many cases not all. But if you need an ally to say I am straight what better way that having an affair with the opposite sex. This totally diverts all suspicions. You get your fiends to cover up for you thinking they are covering up one lie but actually covering up the lie they know nothing about.

The coverup of an ongoing affair or Anonymous hookup will always start with some type of change or many changes in the partner. Now you will have some idea what to look for in the future or now.

As stated earlier if you think or feel there is something going on your instinct is probably correct. We all have hidden or true feelings that we can not describe. This is very common and most of the time we try to hide our feelings so people do not think we are crazy. I suggest that you act on the feelings and do your research be nosy if you want to know. And if you do not care and the status quo is good for you then let it drop. Just by purchasing this book you are more than curious. You know there is a problem and this book just may bring it to the surface.

It is honestly one of the reason I wrote the book is to help people that need a push to take the next step of realization. If it helps you understand that you may have a reason for concern, and that your partner may not have any control over the situation either.

STORY 6: WISCONSIN FIRST TO LAST

– XXX –

FIRST TIME WITH THEM

In Wisconsin I met a couple Tony and Rita, "o" Sweet Rita many times when a guy says his wife has a sweet pussy its a figure of speech well not in this case. I arrived at the house chitchatted for a few minutes and Tony said he had to go upstairs and he would be right back, Rita said come with me we walked out to a garden room all glass and there was a massage table she undressed me and then she undressed. I said should we wait for Tony, no he will be fine all this talking has made me so horny she said.

She jumped on the table spread her legs and said get to it! So I did as I was told I got down on my knees there just happened to be a homemade foot stool just perfect height. I started licking her pussy and instantly knew that I had never had tasted anything like it. Truly sugar sweet, like eating cotton candy the best pussy I had or have ever had. I was into it she shot a squirt into my mouth as she came like nothing I tasted. She said don't stop your the best ever I was buried in between her legs and look over and a massive cock was being stroked inches from my face Tony was there all 9 thick inches of it. I grabbed him put it in my mouth he said Rita damn he is good. I know she said let me have more of him.

For thirty minutes back and forth then he would stick it in her pull out let me lick the sweet nectar from his cock. She had cum 8 times and then said ok now Ron fuck me I asked him if it was ok sure go for it. I was so excited I put it in her didn't last long I said I am cuming she said fill me baby! I did as I was told, squirt after squirt then Tony said ok move, let me unload I pulled out he went in he shot his load making her moan from the pulses then he got down and sucked all the cum out of her. He went up to her mouth and snowballed with her till two loads of cum were shared by both. Rita asked me while she relaxed could I eat her one more time. Hell yes she came again and again, never had any lady cum so many times and so often without saying enough. I got hard again and Tony bent over sucked me while I was eating her and then I fucked her again but as I was getting ready to cum she had been sucking Tony's cock she said feed me your load I hurried to her mouth and just made it before another huge load pulsated from my hard cock. She didn't miss a drop. We went to the living room and Tony still bearing his huge hard cock Rita and I together sucked him till he shot it into her mouth.

Ron Garrett

Second Time

It was a work day in Wisconsin but I so wanted to see Tony and Rita again and to make it work out I left home at 2 am drove to Wisconsin to play before my 9am meeting. Tony and I set it up without Rita knowing. I arrived at their house and quietly went in where Tony and I made our way into the bedroom I crawled under the sheets and started eating her. She said "Tony O my feels good", but she opened her eyes and Tony's big cock was an inch from her mouth she pulled back the covers and said you guys lol. Then we all sucked and fucked till exhaustion he would fuck her I would fuck her we all took turns with each other for two hours finally afterwards she had squirt 10 times and couldn't do it again. Showered and still was 15 minutes early for meeting.

Last Time

The last chapter of my adventure with Tony and Rita. Due to loosing my job of 20 years I never saw them again. I will not repeat everything but we did add one more position to our sex party. Rita whispered to me Tony has tried many times to fuck my ass he is just too big. But it will excite him if you would can you? Yes baby I will try. So to surprise Tony she got on his big cock and I was on top from behind we were taking turns going in and out of her pussy then I lubed up and fingered her ass to open he pulled out without knowing I put it in her she let out a deep moan he thought I hit her G spot but then she said ok Tony put it in. He did and to his surprise he felt my cock and I could feel his cock getting even bigger before he said anything. Tony said it was the best fuck of his life feeling my cock through the walls of her pussy. When we came it seemed to last for ever just kept cuming and cuming. We rolled off her and the cum oozed out covering the sheets. She called the next day to say cum was coming out her ass all night! Well if it were to be the last time what a way to go out. I will never forget them, her truly sweet pussy and his huge beautiful cock.

And a footnote one of the nicest if not the nicest couple I have ever met in my entire life.

7

OPEN RELATIONSHIP

What is an open relationship? There are several different explanations or answers to the question. Basically the answer is when a couple is open to allowing their partner to have other sex mates. To dive deeper it can be with or without them being present. And this is totally up to the couple. Many are only open if they are playing together. While others take a don't ask don't tell approach. And still others want to know when, where and what you did. But they have to know. So Open is basically you can mess around with others given certain criteria.

Truly Open Relationship is all about trust and lack of jealousy. Very hard to get to the non-jealous point in an open relationship. But once you and your mate truly understand love, then sex is not as confined as many think. You have to understand Sex is Not Love. Not even close but all too often they get lumped together and that is where couples start having serious problems in their relationship. Not saying that monogamous relationship are not great because for a vast majority of the population that is the only way to be in a committed relationship. But there are from what I see and feel about 20%-25% that would have an open relationship if their partner was willing. But also the vast majority are closeted they are called cheaters. Because they can't get what they desire they find it in extra marital affair.

The affairs will range as a Long Term on going affair, which often leads to one of the two falling in love and that will add an entirely new set of problems. To a Hit it when you can with the same person not a relationship but just sex. Then you get to the majority and that will be the Anonymous sex when you can with who you can. Definitely not love and definitely not long term thus the reason for the Anonymous being so popular is the fact that there is no calling the other person, there is no names in most cases. But if you truly like it you can get a number or way to contact them and do it again. But knowing that it will run its course and you will not want to be with them again no matter how good because you need and want something new. Remembering these are not relationships but just Anonymous hookups.

Anonymous is popular for another reason and that is the lack of commitment. Anonymous is not only popular with married or partnered people but just as many of them are single. They just don't want the pressure, the cost, the going home without sex and spending maybe hundreds of dollars on the date. The other person not being their type. The other person falling in love and creating problems. The drama is too much so they just go for what ever they can get when they can get it. With Anonymous sex all of the above is not an issue. You get your rocks off and you are done. And if you are having a really good day that may happen two are three times in a few hours. The best thing that Anonymous sex has going is you can be as non-committal as you want. You owe them nothing and they owe you nothing and you both understand why you and they are there. This may sound like a terrible way to live but it is honest and you have to wonder how many people that feel trapped in a marriage or partnership feel this way? They cannot afford to get out of the situation so feeling trapped only adds to the frustration level, which in turn leads to resentment. And that resentment leads to easy Anonymous sex.

As I digressed now getting back on point. Once you start in an open relationship it is hard if not impossible to go back to the old way of life. If more partners would be more understanding the divorce rate would drop by 25% and attorneys would be delegated to chasing ambulances. And the reasoning of the number is totally hypothetical. But if I am correct with my estimate of number of people that have cheated. Then it would hold true if many divorces happen due to lack of the kind of sex you want then this number should be fairly accurate.

How to approach the angle of open relationship with your spouse or partner this will be or could be the most honest but unprepared conversation you will ever have with anyone. There is no way to determine where it will go you may be totally surprised that they say I was thinking the same thing.

Not a relatively good idea to jump into the entire thought process at first, most people need a gradual easement into the new life style of ideas. I will tell you it is much better to let it be the other person idea. The more you fantasize about it and then draw them into the thinking the better off you will be in the long run. For example you are a male and love sucking but your wife doesn't know then once she is on board to making her feel great and it is all about her it will be time to gently proceed. You will need several casual sessions to get her use to playing well with others. After that works let her run the show ask her if there is anything else she would like to see or do and that you are willing to make her fantasy come true. Maybe suggest you really want to taste her pussy after another guy has made love to her. This suggestion will be the start of the conversation we'll not conversation but action. Talk about when there are three of you it is hard not to rub cock to cock or even have the other cock touch you but you are ok with it. For the most part it will be a point that she will understand.

Then once that point is considered it is time for the next move which is to find a guy willing to let you suck him and tell the wife he wants you to do it because it turns him on. Ironically wife's find it harder to say no to strangers than their own husband. You will need to protest just a little but not too much then kiss and have the cock slide between you making her lips the focal point. That is one suggestion, this entire book is open to help both sides of a relationship. Help each person understand that what they are feeling is natural and there is no right or wrong way there just is. But if you want to stay in your relationship this is one way to assist in the process.

You will see in the next XXX story number 7 that sometimes it happens by accident and with no planning on your part or if the planning and setup maybe reversed maybe your partner had the feeling of doing it or has done it and I was totally naive to understand that two can play the game. I truly wondered if she had, had affairs while I was out doing it maybe she was doing it also.

STORY 7: MY WIFE'S IDEA

– XXX –

I was at another Chefs convention in Washington DC and I took my wife so she could see a part of the country she had never seen while I was in the meetings she could relax explore the city or what ever wives do when husbands or wives are at Chef conventions. After a long day of seminars and endless platitudes of Chef this and Chef that, "How Great Thou Are" bullshit I was exhausted. If you have never been around a Chef you may not understand they are the most self indulgent, egotistical, narcissistic group of professionals in the world. Literally the air in the room was thin because when they walked in the room they sucked it in. Sorry I digress. But we had one day off and she had without me knowing contacted her cousin which I had never met, and she had a new husband to show off. She had agreed to meet downtown at the Mall in DC.

It was great both very nice and as we walked and talked near the reflecting pool at the Mall between the two famous monuments they were telling the story how they met and married. Then we decided to get something to eat a the local food court, I need to make some phone calls for work and asked if I could step away for 15-20 minutes. I got the reluctant approval and did just that. Upon returning my life changed. My wife said "you tell him about it" to her cousin I said "tell me about what?" Go ahead tell him well as is aways the case my former wife could not wait and she told the story. "Well Suzzie and Keith go to swingers clubs and asked if we wanted to go". "What the hell that's not anything what I thought you were going to say" I said. We all laughed and then I said well what do you think? to my wife. Well I was shocked beyond belief when she said "it would be fun to go watch to just see what goes on" and there it was. The elephant in the room the words could not be taken back her secrets reviled she has been thinking about fucking someone else. It was awkward from that point forward with the newlyweds. But once going back to our room at the Sheraton Hotel and Convention Center, I asked "were you serious about going" she said "well it my just spark up our life watching others doing it in public like that". I said I am game if she was and it was done just like that. We fucked before going to the dinner that evening and it was a honestly good fuck the first one in a while. She was crazier than normal and got on me with her big tits hanging telling me to suck them suck them hard. We did not make love we Fucked. I could tell she was fantasizing about others and so was I.

About a week went by with no talk of the swingers club and then out of no where Suzzie called today and wants us to make a trip to Pennsylvania. "when" I asked. "next weekend" she said. Wow soon how can we make it work I asked. I already have she said I booked a flight they will pick us up we will be staying at there new house just two nights and back home Sunday night. She said I called MaryAnn my group secretary and made sure you were not booked on Friday. These were the days when a group secretary basically had everyones schedule and could keep track of all of the people that had desks in the office. Damn you must really want to see the "Hershey Chocolate Factory" which she looked at me like I was crazy she had no idea it was made in Pennsylvania, she said no we are going with them Friday night to the swingers club about two hours from their house. I just laughed and said I already figured that out.

We arrived about noon and when to their new house. It was a very nice large four bedroom ranch style home. We had a relaxing time a few of their adult children were there so we could not talk about our adventure. Finally about five pm we left because the club was several hours away. The ladies had a change of cloths because we could not leave the house dressed like hookers. On the drive we found out that the one older son was seen at the club one night. When they recognized the sons car in the parking lot, so they drove all that way and did not go in. But the new husband got two blow jobs on the way home.

The building was much larger than I expected. We went down a large set of steps and paid our fee, dropping our marked bottle of liquor at the bar and sat at a table. Most of these type of clubs do not have a liquor license. The ladies changed in the ladies room wow hot tits hanging out.

There were over a hundred and fifty people this club, they did allow for single men to attend. Many of the clubs are couples only. My now ex-wife had her eye on a single guy at one of the other tables. To tell the truth I was a little jealous but then thought back how many guys have I sucked and the jealousy slowly disappeared. Suzzie and her husband then took us on a tour of the facilities. It was much larger inside than I would have ever thought. Three hall-ways with individual rooms with beds and doors. Two very large rooms with glass so others could watch the group action going on in each room. We stopped and watched eight people doing every sexual position possible a lot of lady on lady action with the men helping them out. Four ladies were on a kingsize bed eating each other and the husbands taking turns fucking the ones that had their ass in the air. Occasionally one of the men would go up and let the ladies suck them and then back to fucking their pussies. We all got hot and hard watching the action. Our tour continued and finished about ten minutes later. We saw several large rooms with glory holes lined up on one wall. And around the corner we saw an open room with no doors and two opening with two large kingsize beds next to each other. We when back to the bar and in a few minutes Suzzie and her husband were gone. I said well lets go walk around. We again stopped at the window rooms where there was a large crowd gathered. The same group was still there huge hard-ons still in use on the hot pussies. These guys were hard for over forty five minutes. Damn what stamina! I reached under my wife's dress and started fingering her in front of every one she finally said let's walk. We peeked into one of the glory hole rooms but no cocks were there. And we finally went around the corner and she was pulled into the open group room she started rubbing the guys crotch and got him good and hard.

Two guys surrounded her and were playing with her pussy and tits. I decided not to watch and went for a walk. Came back and she saw me and told the two guys she was going to walk around but would be back. On our second trip walking around the one guy motioned for her she said something in his ear and he motioned for her to go into the glory hole room. She told him to go on the other side and we would go in this other side. We closed the door and she said "is it ok?" and I said "yes go for it".

About ten seconds later a nice thick cock came through the hole. She started sucking it and to my amazement another big cock came through another hole. I thought damn I want that one but knew she would know if I started sucking it, but I could not resist it I started stroking it. I did not think she could see me but she stopped sucking and I said "I wanted to make sure he did not leave so you could suck him too". She bought it and then she started sucking him also, going back and forth sucking and stroking them both. I was behind her rubbing the back of her head. The first guy blew his load all over my pants. And she stood up and got on the bed and said fuck me. So I took off my cloths and we fucked like teenagers. She was screaming out fuck me harder. She came two times during the session. I came and we dressed and went into the hall where several people were gathered a bit embarrassing. And we both went to the bathroom cleaned up and met again at the bar. Had a drink but her cousin was still not back. She went over to a table and then two other guys with their wife watching stood up and I could not see but I assume they pulled down her dress top because one of the wives said very nice. And I saw his head disappear assuming he was sucking her tits. The one wife said she had to go to the bathroom and asked my wife to join her. They were gone a very long time she did not say and I did not ask but I assume the lady ate her pussy in the bathroom/dressing room. I was on the way to the bar for another drink for her and I overheard the wife said to the table "I think I ate his cum and they all laughed".

Her cousin was still not back so she said do you want to walk around I said no go I will be here looking at the sights. Again she was gone about thirty minutes, I never asked her what happened but later a couple saw her at the table and stopped and said thanks. And now it was almost eleven and her cousin sat down and asked if we were having a good time I said "yes one more than the other and we laughed". I was ready to go, fortunately they said they were ready to go and we did.

The trip home was very entertaining. They said they were in three different rooms but did not go into details. My wife told them about sucking the two guys but nothing more. And then told how I fucked her hard, about then she stopped and unzipped me and sucked me off in the back seat. Only coming up to answer the questions the front seat was asking. Then her cousin said don't get any on the seats. She leaned up and said I will swallow. About then the cousins head was gone. We joking said don't get any on the seats she lifted up and said never. It was a trip of a life time. Even though we went to three other swing clubs it never became a regular thing and abruptly stopped as fast as it started.

Once in a swingers club in Chicago my wife was pulled on stage but unfortunately I was at a spot way in the back and could not see what went on exactly. The two that pulled her on stage were a married couple and I stood and could make out that the lady was between my wife's legs as she was sitting on a stool and the guy was directly in front of her moving his hips back and forth. About twenty minutes went by and she came back, I said did he have a big cock? She said it was a little longer than mine but not as thick. Then I asked was the wife good at eating your pussy no reply to that question.

She said lets go for a walk and we did running into a very handsome man that was walking with a different couple. He stopped and asked us to join them she declined. I said why no reason but she kept going back to watch the three of them fuck and I know she did not want me to see her in action. This was part of her life that she truly did not want any witnesses. Ironically she was a Jehovah's Witness, always makes me laugh.

8

WHO'S TO BLAME

lame the oldest game in the world. When we were young we blamed our siblings. As we got older we blamed our work mates. When we got married we blamed our partner. And when it comes to a lifestyle differential, the truth is neither, are innocent. Yes one person may show their true colors but is it really anyones fault. The simple answer is NO. Some would argue this is not a choice it is how we were programmed at an early age and nothing no matter what would have changes the outcome of the situation. What is to blame is to let society dictate how we act and who we are. None more than me are guilty of letting social norms and family dictate to me how I should be and and should act. And totally due to outside influences we go the direction that everyone thinks we should. There in lies the problem.

If it weren't for outside influences and people could be who they really are the world would have a lot less hurt and disappoint. It is impossible to hold it in, bottle it up and act like you don't have these feelings. Yes you can for a while, and maybe along while but eventually you will surface and your true colors will show.

I know multitudes of gay men that were once married to a lady. Equally I know many lesbians that were once married to a man. Ask yourself why? Did they know ahead of time about their tendency toward the same sex? The answer is mostly yes. So why would they follow the norm and get married to begin with to the opposite sex if we knew? There currently is a seismic shift in societal norms. I truly feel that we will have less conventional marriages in the future due to this shift. People do not feel the pressure of following the suggested norm in society as we once did. Equally I know many men that have never been with a women and many women that have never been with a man. Somehow I feel these are the honest ones the ones that maybe had to hide their feelings but never lied to themselves. They were true to their feelings and did not want to harbor internally what they knew was not real. So as not to pass the buck but who is to blame? We all are, for allowing and making people conform to be something they can not live with indefinitely.

Do some people change yes they do and they just slowly drift into a different lifestyle. I met an old man in a porn cinema and he told me his wife of forty years died and he knew he could not replace her but still needed sex occasionally and found it easier to get oral sex from a man, he did not have to work at it. So he started going to porn places get off and go home, laughingly we said cheaper than dinner and with guaranteed results. But this is where we are as a society and people need a place to fill a need, as many of you are saying now well that just is not right. Not right for who? Reminds me of the story of the young man walking along the beach that was covered with starfish and he was picking them up and throwing them back in the ocean. A old man walked by and said look there are thousands of them and you think you can make a difference? The boy picked up a starfish and thew it in and said I did to that one. So when some people go to places it is not that they are perverted but they have a need. So are they truly to blame. I am not saying this is the only reason but there are many that have that need, and thank goodness there are a few to help them.

Which now brings me to the next part of blame. Once we start using sex as a punishment it is over! The second, one partner with-holds it, the other will find it somewhere else, and the path of least resistance will typically end up being the lifestyle they choose. One guarantee it is easier to find men willing to have sex than it is to find women. And due to mens insatiable appetite for sex that becomes another reason people are prone to have same sex relationships or just **anonymous** sex. And the easier it becomes the more we want it and thus starts the vicious cycle of wanting more with different guys. Knowing that guys are willing anytime and any place for the most part, I am shocked that the percent of bi or gay is not higher.

To give a scary example I have a friend who had anal sex with eight different guys in one day and still wanted more. Likewise I know a bottom guy who lost count how many guys entered him in one night at a gay sex club. Lost count at a dozen now some of you just became very discussed. But the question is why? No that is not my live style but as I have stated my goal is to be one hundred per-cent honest so here goes. I probably sucked six or eight guys in the same night. Once we all know what we want we don't stop till we are done or have to go home. One thing about me is I seldom do it to completion and never swallow or allow it to shoot in my mouth. On occasion it has happened but with the over a five hundred guys I have been with I can count on one hand how many came in my mouth. As bad as this will sound I don't do it for them, it is a desire I have yes to make them feel good but only to a point. I owe them nothing and they owe me nothing, there is no feeling of love at-tached it is basic instinct of only getting off and feeling good. And many guys love the servicing of others and it is nothing about the other guy its what we want to do, satisfy our needed.

So the second area of blame comes from us withholding, that turns into something else. When guys have same sex for the first time especially when it happens later in life there is a real metamorphose that happens. Its like if you never travel to see the world you have no idea what you are missing. Well sex is the same until you experience a different more invigorating sexual experience you have no idea what you are missing. And once you get it you can't get enough. And that is when you start to change into a bi guy or person and eventually maybe into a gay guy or person. At this point you are starting to wonder if gay or bi is only about sex. Yes and No for some it all about sex and relationships are secondary. But to other gay men it is no different it is all about the relationship and is basically traditional relationship, except for one difference your partner is the same sex. And many of these relationships in the gay lifestyle are equally as monogamous as straight couples. And there are gay couples that are open but only when the other partner is with them. They don't stray except with each other.

Now for another truth even monogamous gay relationship have cheaters. One of my best friends couples that I have had many encounters with together, and are according to them only play together with no exceptions cheat on each other. So why do people that don't have to cheat because they can get it when ever they want still cheat. Well people no matter how open and loving you are to your partner still have desires that do not include them and the thrill of a new person with only the attention of them singly is still exciting. I am alway amused by the number of guys on websites that say we must be discreet because I am married. Years ago I assumed it was to a woman and now it is fifty fifty if it is a man or woman. Once any of us go down that road it is hard to ever recover and come back to a strictly monogamous relationship. As I have stated many times thus far people for the most part do not or will not change. Once a cheater always a cheater.

With guy and ladies that have bi or gay tendencies there are four choices in confronting the life you want.

1. It Can be an open relationship between the two of you. Where one person doesn't want to know what is going on it just happens outside the marriage or in other words an example of don't ask don't tell.
2. The relationship becomes a mutual exploration of each other's want and desires where you have mutual non judgmental sex where others join you or the other chuck and just watches. But you do it together.
3. You go your separate ways and give up the life you have together.
4. You continue cheating as we just discussed. Even if you are doing the open but the other one knows these types including me still find it hard to tell your partner everything.

I will explore each option but first I will tell you that most marriages **end** because of Fear! Yes, Fear we are afraid to tell the other person our deepest thoughts because we feel that they will not understand. So we hold it in and then the emotions become too much and we cheat or stay so miserable we hate ourselves. Then the hatred turns to resentment and every one is unhappy. Now every little thing becomes an issue. No matter how small, it turns to the other person doesn't care about me. But the fact is that the other person doesn't know what you want because you are too afraid to express yourself honestly, because you feel that they would not understand. And yes such as in my case, my now second ex-wife was a Jehovah Witness and I knew it was never going to work. But there was a time as you saw in other chapters she was willing. But because I didn't comfort her in the way she needed I went back to being closed and unapproachable giving her no credit, that just maybe she would understand.

How can we approach the issue when fear is a huge factor? One is to gently explore what you want such as having her play with your butt hole ever so gently at first then move to the next stage. Always saying how much you love it and it really makes you happy. Encouraging your partner to do more and ask for more also. Doing everything they ask and never judge them. Once you do judge they will shut down and it will be over. As human beings we are not forgiving once turned down we may never ask again twice told no then it is over. And the spiral of looking for something else starts. This is not to say that everyone will turn in to a cock sucking whore but the straying thoughts start. We look at other couples and say I wish I had what they have. Or when friends tell you how exciting their sex is and you start to feel more and more disappointed.

1. The don't ask don't tell relationship has a slim possibility to work especially if you have been married a long time with grown children. Because one member has already decided that sex is over and they can live without it. If that is the case you have a chance because you have been together so long that neither of you are willing to give up what you have and you are more willing to go through the motions and play your part. No one will ever know and basic contentment that sits in as you become long term room mates. You will go through the occasional who's to blame and its your fault but you eventually live in peace. One of my good friends that we hook up is married and has been for

over thirty years but has not had sex with his wife in over ten years. So we get together and make each other happy and he goes home. She knows what he is doing but does not want the marriage to end so they play the game of holidays, friends etc without telling anyone else about their arrangement.

2. Once you decide, after a very long thought process that you may or will join the lifestyle your world will change. I can not predict the outcome of your decision. Because once the cat is out of the bag it may change for your partner they may find that part of the allure was that it was a secret and hiding was part of the excitement of doing what they do. But in all likeli-hood it may save and make a marriage grow. Especially if the open and understanding leads to a more honest life together. The couples that I meet up with have a loving and fantastic re-lationship. They can truly tell each other everything and not be judged. And once that freedom is met it only follows that ev-erything else will become better. It would be fantastic if we can all go through life and say what we really want to say and truly have someone understand us. How liberating to say damn I feel like finding a strange guy and bring him home so we can share or whatever the scenario may be in your life. The good thing is it does not matter because you both understand the needs of the other. So many of the couples that I meet up with tell stories in front of their partner that I could never have told any of my partners. They were so honest they made me blush. And I also felt like I had missed out and was so jealous of what they had because I never did have it.

3. You both decide it is too much and you must depart the relationship too much has happened to put it back together. This is devastating to see a relationship end but if one party or both can not get the feeling back it is much better to leave and start anew than hold anger and resentment for each other for ever. That is not healthy and separation from the situation over time will help, it may never go away but time does heal the wound. The anger you feel for the person needs to go away as quickly as possible because it only holds you back from true happiness. When your life is consumed with hate you will never find love and peace. And maybe long term relationship will never be truly long term who knows, but if you don't open a space in your heart for it to happen then it never will happen.

Many a song has been written about a broken heart and many a tear has been shed from a lost love. That only means that you have the ability to love again. And when you expand your heart your possibilities expand. I see all kinds of angry people in this world from road rage to people that think the worlds owes them something. Wrong the world owes you nothing, and the sooner we realize it the better we will be. What causes that anger is many times family and friends, church, religion, fucking politicians start telling you what you should do and how to pay a person back for hurting you. Really what has that ever helped? When they say two wrongs don't make a right, I totally agree. I truly feel that the world has become a me me me place to live and everyone has a agenda and it has started with how we are used by political parties they have divided us so badly that it is hard to have an opinion and a discussion without everyone getting mad. Stop it, let people voice their option and learn something . For gods sake why is an option only good if we agree with it?

This book is the same, really controversial and many men will not read it because it will uncover their deep dark secret. Well that is not the point the point is to uncover me. I have to discover who I am in the processes.

So if separation is the outcome making it the best fucking outcome it can be. Don't let anyone define you. Discover a new you this goes to each side of the party. There is no reason to think only one side will have a great outcome I truly hope that both sides come out equal that is when everyone wins and grows.

And now for number four. You continue cheating as we just discussed. Even if you are doing the open but the other one knows these types including me still find it hard to tell your partner everything. But the problem being after reading this book your partner now knows. They now are starting to understand more about you and what makes you tick. They are much smarter to your lies and dishonesty. Now hiding in the shadows may no longer be an option. Yes, some of us will still try to coverup and lie because that is how we're made. But finally your partner will hand you this book and say read it was written for and about you. Take the time to finally look deep and ask are you wanting to stay in a relationship or not. Because if we can't be honest now when the door is open to discuss it, we never will be ready. Lying takes a mental toll on us and the time is to relax take a breath and tell the truth. As Adel says in her song Go Easy On Me, they just may but only the truth will get you to your point in life to find out.

STORY 8: BI FRIDAY NIGHT GROUP

– XXX –

There is a place in Park Forest IL were they have two houses one for straight couples and one for Bi couples and select bi/ gay singles. Never went to the straight parties but here are a few stories about the Bi parties. They only allow 10 single bi men the rest bi couples. Upon entering the small loft home, I was warmly greeted by Karen a petite beautify lady . She gave me a warm inviting huge, I paid my $70 and she introduced me to her husband Tim, and told him to give me a tour. There was a DJ area near the entry a small living room area that lead to the back kitchen where there was a bring your own liquor with mixers and glasses they also provided a vast array of food. There was an outside enclosed deck for smokers. A Small separate room with three couches just off the kitchen area. Then to a back bedroom with a king bed and through a wall of curtains was three king mattresses on the floor. And Tim almost forgot to show me the closet where there was two curtains which there was a glory hole. It was right next to the first kingsize bed.

Venturing to the top of the spiral staircase there was one doorway to the right a big room where couples can invite single guys but single guys can not enter if not invited. That room had 6 beds on the floor separated by shear curtains. And at the top of the stairs was an open king bed. The open room also had and a swinging basket at the base of the bed and a fuck table in another part of the room, along with a bathroom and shower.

My first visit was a little scary I was new to open sex where others could see me. There were a lot of firsts at these parties. Being naive I ask what goes on here? Karen told me everything goes on you name it. So I found the room with glory hole I went in and around 2 minutes later a guy put his cock through the hole

I knew exactly what to do so I started going down on it and I was shocked when the curtain opened on my side so I stopped sucking and his wife said it my husband and I want to watch you sucking him. So I started up again going at with vigor. She would go back and forth saying baby do you like it? "He is good"! So hot then she entered my side of the glory hole and pulled up her skirt and said eat it. Then her hubby came over to watch. Then she said lets get on the bed that was next to the booths she lay back and had me eat her and I would take turns going back and forth eating her and sucking him. And when I came up from eating pussy I was looking for his cock to suck but he was sucking a huge black cock so I went back to eating his wife who was truly enjoying the attention. Then lookin up he was on his knees next to his wife with a huge black cock in his ass. The other three beds were full, 8 people 4 guys fucking and/or getting fucked and the other 4 wives and two licking balls and ass while the other two wives were 69 eating each other like starving kittens.

Finally the wife I was eating said fuck me so I did and then another hot lady jumped up on the bed and spread her pussy directly over her mouth, while I fucked her she was eating away. She started to moan and her hubby who was still taking the huge black cock said to me get ready, she's a gusher you have about 10 seconds.

The girl getting eaten said pull out I did and she bent over, with her pussy still in the face of the lady I was eating, took most of the squirt in her mouth. But she still managed to squirt in my face over the other girls head like nothing I had ever seen. I was ready to cum so I asked where she wanted it she said feed him. So I quickly walked around and put it in her husband's mouth and unloaded not a drop was spilt. I have no idea how long it went but after I cleaned up I walked by the room and he was still taking the huge black cock. The two of them were so much fun. That was the only thing I did that night because as soon as I came I left. Not sure why but that feeling came over me, asking myself why did I leave when I was having so much fun.

The next time I visited was the time which I really started to get to know the regulars and one couple in particular. They were older than me but in the best shape of any couple that I have ever met. On their SLS profile you could see they were runners and their body showed. Zero extra fat on either not sure why they liked me a fat guy but they did. They proceeded to tell me she always started the party off when she finished her champaign it was time. He told me if I wanted to be first with her then he would let me know when she was ready and I would be her first. About a half hour later I looked over to him and he nodded and motioned me to go upstairs. A few minutes later they arrived upstairs and she took hold of me and said I understand you want to be first.

Well here is what you are going to get she slid her fingers in and out of her pussy put them in my mouth and said, you better be good. She straddled a sex seat put both feet in stirrups and said your turn. As I started to get down her husband undid his towel hiding a massive thick cock. He said get me wet so I can open her up for you. I did as told and still one of the thickest cocks I have ever done. He was dripping with my saliva and he slid inside her making her moan deeply. He pulled out and said taste it and I did as told without any hesitation. Truly remarkable, then without warning he took my head and forced it between her legs. Saying don't come up until she squirts. I totally did as told and it took me about fifteen minutes but she started to shake and squirm and the eruption happened. She shot on my face I was totally shocked how much she squirted. As soon as I thought she was done he said move and he put his massive member in her and about thirty seconds later she started erupting again. He was soaked and so was I, never leaving my position he had me lick her again. And she screamed I can not take anymore. She quivered for over five minutes as he and I each had a nipple in our mouths. Simply stated she said it was the best combo ever in her life. Every time I went to the club they made me their first one and we were never disappointed each time was just as good as the first. The very last time I went to the club years ago she was exceptionally crazy while her hubby and I was servicing her pussy she was eating every pussy and sucking every cock she could. My count was three pussies and eight loads of cum and still begging for more. Damn he said once a year she gets like this and can't stop.

There was one more couple that I always tried to hook up with when I was able to attend the parties. They were totally different than my other couple she had huge firm natural breast and he was a sub that was told what to do and with whom. I love the way she controlled him and he did not seem to mind. She was a stunning beauty every girl and guy wanted her but she controlled everything. She would dismiss you quickly if you were pushy or in any way she did not like you. She almost sent every single guy packing and wanted nothing to do with them. Not sure why they like me but she loved the way I made sure they were happy. Some times I felt like her pimp she would send me to get her a certain person and mostly not for her but to take care of her husband. One night she had five different guys line up and go at him moving from his mouth to his ass for over an hour he got pounded.

Remembering they were held on a Friday night over two hours from my house and I was still married to my first wife and it was very difficult to get away that often. I managed to hit six times that year out of twelve. Shortly after that I was divorced and went almost every month for a year, before my next marriage. One thing that was different with this party was there was the ten single guys limit allowed. And I thought that was good idea first of all we paid more than the couples and it keep the ratio fairly consistent of three to one, couples vs singles. And between the horny ladies and men all the single guys were very busy. I had to learn how to preform several times during the night and also orally satisfy many people. It was not as easy as you would think it became exhausting. I was not as young as many of the people but what a great group always felt welcome and inviting. The owners of the club on more than one occasion invited me to spend the night with them.....

9

FAMILY AND HOW THEY INFLUENCED ME

Being from a somewhat conservative but a not extremely religious family there were many norms built into everyday life in midwest America. And those were often the normal situation of many people born in the fifties, nineteen fifty five to be exact. We were vastly approaching the end of the baby boomer cycle but gearing up for more of the cold war. We were about to jump into the middle of the sexual revolution and may would argue totally due to one man that dared to shake his hips on national TV and could only be filmed from the waist up. Elvis may have single handily started the sexual revolution but others kept it alive. As Elvis went into the Army he left behind a culture that would forever change the world. As Elvis was not in the spotlight we started many different revolutions.

We had the British Invasion, Free Love, Folk Rock with deep societal meaning, and all of a sudden the words to a song could start a movement. Music seem to be much more influential years ago than it does now. Dylan would write it down and the world would live it. With lyrics such as "love the one you're with" from Stephen Stills in nineteen seventy, and as musical lyrics was pushing through society there was also an underground movement of Gay bars and nightclubs popping up faster and more and being closed just as fast.

The Mafia ran most of the gay bars especially in New York, and they paid off the politicians and law enforcement to look the other way. Not only did Fat Tony from the Genovese family by the now famous Stonewall bar he converted it to a Gay bar. And He would blackmail rich patrons and threaten to out them. Can not confirm but it is said that he made as much money extorting married men and politicians as he did in the bar. They the gay bars would charge more for drinks and cover charges than a straight nightclub. Not only that, they would dilute the alcohol by fifty percent with water knowing that the customer would not complain. Because homosexuality was mostly still illegal in many parts of the United States The gay bars were basically still underground establishments, and that lead to a situation in New York when finally the Gay people stood up and said were not going to take in anymore. Thus the event in 1969 that will live forever "Stonewall Riots". Named for the riot that took place outside the Stonewall Bar. And the crowd became so large and unruly the Police actually barricaded themselves inside the Stonewall bar for their own protection.

So to say that family influenced me would be an understatement or overstatement depending on how we look at everything going on around us. I remember for Christmas one year my father went to the store got me a cassette player and asked the clerk what is the music teenagers liked and came home with The Rolling Stones. Great choice dad!

The sixties grew the Free Love movement which just grew by leaps and bounds. Gay Pride was just getting started at the same time. And when the two combined with the drug culture the total movement was born. To this day I have never done a drug of any kind. Never needed to, never wanted to. But the sixties were defiantly the experimentation era from drugs to sex.

I lived in a trailer park as a kid and lived a very simple life not being from a big city I missed most of the culture shock that took place . So once figuring out I was Gay or Bi whatever label you want to use, I had a lot of catching up to do and it was not until my late fifties when I came out that I started looking back at the struggles that most gay people when through in their life and dealing with hatred predigest and violence. I missed that in my life so far everyone one has been very understanding and open. But that does not demise what others had to endure. The stories guys have told me are so sad and hateful, I have tears in my eyes now just thinking about it. Many of the men I have met were partnered for thirty or forty years and for the majority of their life together they had to stay in the closet.

And just as it started to be more acceptable for the general public to accept gay people AIDS hit and sent many more people underground. The level of non acceptance grew at an alarming rate. People saying, "good, AIDS are killing the sickos the perverts of society." "The fags should all die." Religious fanatics saying it was Gods way to punish the immoral acts and they deserve to die. It came to a head when major stars such as Elton John came out and then the more that came out the more society started the acceptance again. Elton with his AIDS foundation which was created out of his friendship of Ryan White. Ryan who contracted AIDS from a blood transfusion. He had been dealing with the AIDS for a while and the last time he was admitted to the hospital March 29th, 1990 and died April 8th 1990. When Elton performed Skyline Pigeon at his funeral people were shocked he had white hair and he said later he was near death and needed a reason to live. Battling depression and cocaine and alcohol addiction he had moved to Indianapolis to be near Ryan. Elton said if not for Ryan he probably would have died because of the spiraling use of drugs and alcohol. As sad as Ryans death was it may have saved a super star and countless others due to the foundation that Elton created.

I never came out to my parents as a mater of fact my dad was already dead when my total transformation into my new life started. And I actually told several family members and friends at my moms funeral, maybe not an appropriate place now looking back but when is it a good time? It took a lot and the ones that mattered to me were the most understanding. Anyone else I could care less. Honestly I have no idea how my mother would have handled it but there is a time and place for everything and with her being sick was not the time or the place. But the stories about broken family divided over someone coming out as gay are heart breaking. Loss of inheritance., disowning them etc was very common just a few years back and still for some to this day.

There is a small faction of the gay population that tries to out people by telling family members because they think that being out will help the overall cause. I would never and not really is it anyone else's place except the individuals to tell or not to tell. No one has the right to speak for someone else in this matter. If they are gay and closeted that is their choice not mine or anyone else's business. As my college roommate Grant said "I never came out because I was never in". That is a healthy way of looking at it.

When I came out to my daughter I was living in Puerto Vallarta just finished building my big ocean house and decided I could not take my wife any longer. So two months later I called my daughter and said I need to talk to you and she said go ahead I said no in person. She asked "are you ok" I said "yes I think so" she said "what is it?" I said "no only in person". She said when are you coming to

Tennessee I said let me find a flight and maybe as early as tomorrow. What the hell "are you ok?" I said "yes". So two days later I arrive in Knoxville and was there a few days and said I needed to use her car said ok go with me to work as we were in the drive through of Starbucks she ordered and then looked at me and said "O my god I can't stand it what the fuck is it that you are going to tell me?" I said "well you know the twenty eight year old Spanish teacher that I have have as a "friend", she said "yes omg is she pregnant?" I said "well that would be impossible" then she looked at me and said "Dad are you Gay?" and I said "yes" she said "Thank God I thought you were dying". And that was my coming out to her.

Now my only struggle about my gay/bi life is with my grandchildren. I have not told the thirteen year old and the seven year old would not understand anyway. The Thirteen year old knows I am writing the book and said he wants to read it when it is finished. Well that will be interesting when that day comes. But for not they are the only people that I have not totally told about my life and as I said there is a time and a place and soon will be both..

STORY 9: CHICAGO THEATER COUPLES ROOM

$-$ **XXX** $-$

There was a great place called "15th Street Bookstore" near Chicago. Book store with video booths, private mixed bathhouse and a theater with a back room. When I did not have much time I would stop in arcade suck through the glory hole or get sucked. And get back to work but one night when I was working in the area and staying in a nearby hotel I went to the theater and a couple was sitting in the couples only section of the theater. She caught my eye and she finally came over to me, a hot 25 year old blond with a very hot lean husband. She asked if I liked eating pussy I said yes. Will you do it on the examination table. The table which was a real doctors examination table located up to the right of the screen but totally out in the open. Sure I would love to.

So she nods at hubby and we all three went hand in hand to the table she undressed and put feet in stirrups I went down on her young pink and very warm pussy, immediately she started to moan loud causing the entire theater to gather round. She was sucking every guy jacking them and girls were all over her tits one girl jumped up and put pussy in her face. Her husband was totally nude with a raging huge cock which I looked over and just went for it. His young hot beautiful body was more than anyone could have wanted. I felt that if he were not bi he would push me away but instead he was so excited he got his wife's attention baby look. I spend the next 15 minutes eating her hot pussy and sucking his cock. He said I am going to cum so I grabbed a girl that had crawled between my legs and was sucking my cock and told her to take his load she did just like a trooper. Then she stood up and shared the load with her husband who was getting sucked by another older guy. I went right back on my guy till he was rock hard again and said he wanted fuck his wife. So I moved giving space with my face next to them and from time to time he would pull out and let me have me lick her hot juices from his cock and back in pounding her like a cheep whore. This went till I was so exhausted he finally shot the next load in her but she was so busy sucking and eating she didn't notice. He then wanted me to unload in her too so I put my still rock hard cock in the very sloppy pussy and unloaded adding to the already fully loaded hole. He said are you all unloaded yes move he went down and ate both loads out of her while she moaned and bucked like a crazy woman. Damn sometimes you get more than you could ever expect and this was one of the nights that I thought could not get any better.

We all got dressed and exchanged numbers but we never contacted each other. Exhausted now she kissed me on the cheek and I headed to the bathroom to try to clean the nights sex off of me. I thought it was time to head to my hotel but on my way out I noticed several guys lining the hallway of the arcade so I thought it won't hurt to take a quick look. Even though had cum two times I was still intrigued on what was going on so I entered into a booth started to close the door and a young black guy stopped the door and said want some company, of course I said ok not as enthusiastic as I would have been earlier in the evening. He closed the door and then I noticed I had picked the booth with two glory holes one on each side he said what do you like to do, without hesitation I said suck cock. So I sat on the chair and he suddenly opened the door made a hand gesture and closed door I thought nothing of it. Unzipped his pants and hauled out a perfect piece of manhood. Soft thick and about 8 inches I hit the jackpot again I thought. I touched and smelt it looking for any signs of sores or anything like that was really going to tell me if he had any disease or not, and it was perfect so I would tell myself. A second later it was in my mouth enjoying the musty sexy smell only black guys have. He got perfectly hard and swelled in my mouth. With eyes closed I made mouth love to him and he tapped me on the head and asked if I would like to take care of his friends and I said well not sure there is room. He pointed to the glory holes and then I noticed the other two rock hard cocks were gleaming through so I moved to my knees and would move from one side of the booth to the other this went on for over 30 minutes I was truly exhausted he said do you swallow I said sorry but no I don't and he said ok no problem. He leaned down and said something to each of his friends and then opened the door to the booth both of the other Big Black Cocks appeared in the door way and I sucked all three while a group of many guys watched.

My first guy said he was ready to blow and I moved off and with out hesitation one of his friends bent over and took his load. While he was sucking down every last drop I was sucking him. Then he said I am ready too and I moved the other guy bent over and took his load and I knew what to do so I move to his cock and started sucking him till he finished enjoying the nectar of another then it was his turn and my first guy like we had rehearsed the order bent over and took his load. I stood up with weak knees or should I say they helped me up and said omg that was fantastic. I walked out with a smile that nothing could erases one of the best evenings of my life and I knew it would be hard to ever feel so satisfied and so exhausted all at the same time.

10

CAN YOU CHANGE THEM?

Can you change them? That is not the real question is it? The real question is do they want to change. After living a life outside the given societal norm there is a thrill associated with it that can not be understood by many. Even people that read this book will be slightly or greatly disgusted in parts of it. And to assure you this is G rated compared to the real underground Sex clubs that exist around the world. I have never explored the True Underground but just may in the next book.

When someone is living a life of lies, distrust, uncommitted, unsafe, pure excitement, fun, exhilarating, liberating, mind altering and possibly disease filled, and still does it, is there a chance they will stop? There are all the feelings rolled into one that is what the person feels at different times.

They feel like a **lier,** while they can't or won't tell the truth and that lie haunts them in many cases before and after. When I came out of the closet I was one of the guys that had a family, daughter wife, grandchildren etc and I still did it and I hated myself for it but not enough to stop. In some ways it made me better and in many ways it made me worse. I would find excuses not to be with family because of work, well work was only a small reason the other was that I wanted to play on the side and needed an easy reason to be out of the house. So a note to employers as well as partners. If your mate is gone a lot for work and insisted on staying over at work and telling their partner at home, work made him do it they are covered work will never know what he says at home and vise versa. Work is the perfect cover if they are having a hidden underground life. Most years I would spend over one hundred nights away from home in a hotel. The fact that my job covered seven states helped but in reality I would guess that if I wanted to do a better job of scheduling my time I could have cut the number by half. Thus my addiction was costing my employer money needlessly. Even though during the work day I totally busted my butt and after work would many times work through the night it was that one hour that I was not working that created my overnight stays away from home. I was not and still not a guy that hangs around those places all day and night normally in and out within a hour of time. The exception is the hotel room sex parties.

Distrust not only do others start to distrust you but you start to distrust yourself. If you get a passing glance you start to worry if they know something about you. Did they see you get out of your car at the porn cinema? This starts to turn into paranoia and every-where you turn there is one more thing that makes you think. It is one thing to have an office affair, somehow everyone finds out and says nothing. We had a dietitian that was doing one of the outside sales guys and she thought know one knew. We all knew but chose not to ever say anything it was more fun watching what happened than letting the cat out of the bag. Then there was other times when only close friends knew about the extra marital affairs.

There was a sales guy at work that was having an affair with a customer, quick side story because it is so damn funny. He was doing her in the kitchen of a school and all the lights were off but the door was not locked. In walked the UPS man he acted like he did not see a thing but went on his way and dropped off the package at the front office came back through by that time they were done and he was on his way back to work or they were hiding can't remember exactly. The salesman later in the day was calling on another customer a bar while taking the order from the owner the sales person looked up and thought o shit. In walked the same UPS guy, he made the delivery the salesman thought good he is leaving. And then he turned around and walked up to the owner and him and started telling the story of walking in on two fucking on the stainless steel table at the school. He had no idea he was telling one of the people that was on the table. I still think it is my favorite stories. So when it comes to distrust or any of the other feelings gays and bi's do not have a monopoly, straight affairs are equal in every respect except for societal norm.

The feeling of being **uncommitted** in a cheaters mind is somehow easier to justify because they feel as many people do that monogamy is not possible, for them anyway.

Many times you have read that you can not change them and I will believe as long as I live you can not change them. There maybe a few percentage that will change but the general majority will not. They won't change because they don't want to change and if they don't want to change then how do you think you can change their mind. You think because they have a marriage and children etc that will make them change it will not. The need for Anonymous is more controlling than anything else. They will say what ever they need to make you think they will change but change they will not.

One of the greatest lessons from this book is never assume you are special and because of you they will change. They may love you with all their heart but in their heart they know the answer change will be the next lie. They will do what ever it takes but as soon as the chance happens they will revert back to what they truly and always will be Anonymous.

STORY 10: AFTERNOON GAY NUDE PARTIES

– **XXX** –

Up to 50 men gathered together in a peaceful relaxing setting in a home, at a private pool or large condo. It is a members only club yearly membership fee of twenty dollars and cost $7 each event. The house parties were organized by an older couple and had a mixture of a few twenty somethings, a few thirty somethings, and a few 80 to cap off the assortment but mostly fifty and sixties. The events range from old movies, pool parties, Holiday party but all end up as sex parties. There are several groups like this in the area of Fort Lauderdale Florida. Once entering the home you payed your fee and then you were required to undress and put your cloths in a bag. The only thing you could have on is a towel and socks. Even in this settings no means no, but rarely happened.

Upon my first visit to the club, I didn't understand that as you walk around you will expect to be fondled, groped, sucked and more. But back then being shy walked around and to my surprise walked into a bedroom where 14 guys were piled on and around the bed. Walking around the bed a mouth from under the pile emerges and clamps on my cock. I Pumped his mouth and was almost ready to cum and another guy said enough let me have it and he graciously obliged releasing my cock and the other guy taking it all the way down and seconds later I exploded in his mouth. And I hear the voice say bitch I was working hard for that and you took it from me. We all laughed and then out of know where a guy wrapped his arms around me and went to his knees, I felt a hot tongue go in my ass. Looking over my shoulder seeing a very hot lean young guy that was lapping and eating my man pussy like a dog in heat. I bent over into the pile of men on the bed and let him have as much fat ass as he wanted. I got hard again and he noticed then turned me around and started sucking my cock and balls. Several guys moved so I could lay down to enjoy it all. At that moment another young man was standing near the edge of the bed so I immediately took him in my waiting mouth. Sucking all eight inches of his thick man-hood. The same guy that had earlier took my load whispered in my ear can I please have his load. I nodded yes, and I thought thank god because I don't swallow. And I knew the old guys would be mad if they missed a young man's hot creamy load. A minute later the guy sucking me raised me up and was once again eating my man pussy alternating between cock, ass and balls. About that time I knew my guy was tensing up getting closer and closer to releasing the sperm in my mouth I looked up at him and he knew that I was asking if he was ready. He said I am going to cum! I grabbed the guys head next to me and shoved his cock down his throat just in time for the erup-tion. He pushed his huge cock all the way causing the other guy to gag but my young guy didn't stop he just kept squirting. There was so much, the older man could not swallow fast enough and much of it ended up on my chest. Finally the guy pulled out of his mouth and collapsed next to me. Talking to me saying that was without a doubt the best BJ ever.

As we were talking the other guy was just finishing me off. I told the guy I was talking to that I was going to cum again as soon as I said it he grabbed the other young guy's head and forced him all the way I was bucking like a bronco in to his mouth. I whispered don't hurt him he said it was ok it was his husband. I smiled and said lets exchange numbers. I went and rinsed off took a walk and everywhere I looked guys were fucking, sucking and eating ass.

The extremely old guys, two of them with walkers were having the time of their life grabbing every young guy that walked by, remember everyone was younger. At one time in his life the one guy must have had a huge cock it was still six inches long hanging soft and I found out he was soon to have his ninetieth birthday. The guys had been together for almost seventy years according to the one person.

These parties were also hosted by many guys with house and pool and for hours on end they would eat, then get in the pool have fun, play till they came and get out and drink. Then they would repeat over and over. The bedrooms of the house were also busy with guys that were not interested in the outdoor action. Then there were the large group of lookie-loo's they sat in the living room over looking the pool and I truly think the old queens were just there to talk about the other people. Somehow making themselves better than the others because they were not partaking of the debauchery.

I have said this many times but there is not a bigger group of hypocrites in the world than gays. I am in the group so I know of what I say. For a group that is suppose to be All Inclusive just try disagreeing with them and see how included you feel. I have written about this but every time I think of it I am saddened. They say all the right things but their actions for the most part are totally opposite.

One thing that must be said about every group that I ever attended is that everyone was respectful of the owners stuff. I never saw as mess or never heard of anything missing. When you have a group of fifty or more guys unsupervised you would expect something to go amiss. So with pride I must say as far as I know you could not invite a better group of honest people. They may be caddy but they are honest caddy. Everyone sincerely appreciates the fact that others are willing to open their homes up to so many people that they know and don't know.

The one thing that still makes me wonder is the age of the people had no idea that many guys in there eighties could still perform and many of them well out perform me multiple times. I would not expect there are nearly as many females in that age group that do it or do it as often like this, I am truly always shocked. I could have under estimate them also you will have to let me know. Maybe I should take a trip to the Villages and see for my self.

11

TRAVELING MAN

As I mentioned prior in the chapter on how to tell if your partner is cheating with Anonymous I mentioned travel and over night stays. The other side of that is Vacation Travel there are many guys that will base their vacations on how many hookups they think they can get while traveling. This can happen with or without their partner. And you say who would base a vacation on how active the hookups are, based on a website. I guarantee you that if you have a player partner they are doing the research and looking how close they will stay and where the action is.

They are mapping the distance and figuring how long they can sneak away unnoticed. How close the local porn theater is, and checking google to see when the busy times are going to be on average this will dictate how they suggest to their partner when to do certain things. You will notice things like I booked you a massage for noon on Wednesday. Normally until now you thought my husband is so thoughtful. Now you may know, he was actually booking you away for two hours so he can have play time. And if that goes well you will also get a gift of pedicure and manicure etc as the week proceeds. Anonymous players always have a reason and alternative agenda. I truly hate to sound so callus but reality is reality. Obviously this is not to say that every good deed done by a partner has a motive but to the true Anonymous player it is true a huge percent of the time.

When traveling for vacation there will be in increase interest in the area you stay and the partner will have more input than is normal especially if they are new to the lifestyle. You will find almost every location there is an underground sex business. And if its not a theater, porn store, swingers club, bathhouse, parks, even many colleges and universities. At almost every college or university there will be at least one if not more bathroom with glory holes or out of the way location where guys hookup. This may be shocking to you for the first time reading this but they are out there and abundant.

Its no different than the bathrooms at Home Depot and Lowes if you look online you will find multiple ads for guys to meet in these locations. I remember for years there was a glory hole in the bathroom at a grocery store in Puerto Vallarta. It was entertaining to watch the guys come in with wives and head directly to the bathroom. There was alway a guy in there ready to service mostly white guys for a few pesos. Guys would pass twenty or fifty pesos through the hole typically a young Mexican would service him. While the wife was filling the cart the husband was filling something else.

So the moral of this story is you, will be shocked where and when an Anonymous hookup will or could take place. So it only goes to speculate that everything has an alternative motive for people that are focused on the lifestyle. In looking back my gay partner and I based two European trips on sex. We knew where every bathhouse was and when their busy times and day. We researched every bar weather they had dark rooms or not, porn theaters etc. This is a way of life for many not all gay guys the focus is on sex first and everything else is secondary. So when you find out that your partner is basing their decisions on the lifestyle you will no longer be shocked.

STORY 11: EUROPEAN TRIPS

– **XXX** –

Bathhouses, Bars with dark rooms, porn theaters, sex clubs etc. Europe has them all and wrote the book on many for the gay life style. Even though I have not explored everything Europe has to offer after three trips I have a basic understanding. I must confess I have not been to any of the Underground Sex Clubs. These are the fetish clubs that exist all over Europe but many tell me Germany has cornered the market. But many other European countries are equally as open.

I will start in Paris at the Bathhouse basically a three level bathhouse in what I will call a downtown narrow walkway mall. There are businesses, restaurants etc with a narrow enclosed passageway between them and at the back side of the walking mall is the bathhouse. Euro Men's Club first level ground lockers, showers, coffee and beverage bar along with lockers and sauna. This floor had some action but nothing like the other two floors. One level down was a hallway with approximately a dozen rooms and one dark or should I say very dark room at the end of the one hallway. In making my way into the dark room with my partner I immediately lost him in the maze of men. Being a young tall and very handsome dark complected guy with a huge member he did not last long. They found him and before leaving the confines of the dark room he had fucked three guys blew two others and got sucked off by three other guys. I on the other hand sucked one and got sucked by an old guy normally not my type at all but he knew what he was doing.

After I came I left the confines of the room on to more of the journey. My partner was in the room for at least one more hour. I was down in the pool when he caught up to me wanting to kiss me I declined no way after what he was doing with lord know who, was I in the mood to kiss him. That was the first hour of the six hours we spent there. I said hey I found a theater and he took a quick look around stopping two times to suck two different guys and finally made our way to the theater which was a stair step of wide almost beds three levels high. A guy came to me and started sucking me and I looked over and he had two old guys he was sucking one and another was sucking him. I was getting close to cumming again so I asked my young guy if I could do him before I came. I had not seen his massive cock until he brought it up and at full attention was at least ten inches and thick as a pop can. Maybe the largest one that I ever attempted to service. With all my will I was able to get about four inches into my mouth and not only the largest but the most uncomfortable cock I had ever tried to suck. My jaw was almost displaced but I gave it the old college try for about five minutes and I finally said ok babe finish me off he pulled out and went down and sucked every drop from the tip of my cock. Easily my cock was one forth the size of his and he said wow what a load. Its always nice to get a complement when you know they are just being nice. But contrary to popular belief many of the French were very nice.

Later while on break from the action I saw the same guy in a room with the door open he was balls deep into a guy three times his age. I have no idea how the skinny old man could take all of it but he did. I watched the young guy for about two minutes went for a long walk about fifteen minutes and walked back by and he was still getting it hard and fast. No idea how long it went on but the old guy was getting the best fucking he had ever had I was sure of that. With a cock so big it was almost fist size.

Making my way back to the showers and then to the pool where I waited almost an hour because obviously he had found others to entertain. He made his way after the shower to the pool and we chatted and coming down the stairs he said o my god I will be back and he was off again he walked up to this old guy with huge hanging balls they started talking and then they were gone pass the pool to another area of individual booths there were four hallways and at the end a large room with about 8 rooms and sitting area.

I got tired of the pool and made my way to see if there were anything I happened to be missing and heard him in a room and he opened the door saw me at the end of the hall way and motioned for me to come to him. He said the guy wanted to suck me while he fucked him and I entered the room very attractive big old guy my partner got behind him and I sat on the bench and the old guy went to work on me while he was getting pounded from the back side he was truly enjoying getting it from both ends so to speak. He got me hard again and was excellent at going on it not to hard because this would be third time in as many hours and for me that is a lot. Knowing this would also be my last time of the day because I was exhausted already. He was getting a real pounding for some reason more aggressive than normal he took it and wanted more. I got ready to cum again and I told him he said feed me and I unleashed another load he gaged and went right back for every drop. I said ok boys I will leave you alone and went to the showers for the third time.

When my partner made his way back to me again I asked how

many times have you cum he said six and counting. We both really needed to rest, finally taking a nap on the pool lounge chairs. I woke and he was still napping. I took a walk around finding a beautiful young guy by himself in the theater sitting down next to him I put my hand on his towel rubbing his leg ever so slowly and the more I gently caressed him the more of a tent he was making with his towel. As the tent grew also did my curiosity and with the grace of a swan my hand ventured under the towel to find a perfect eight inches of manhood. I started kissing his body and slowly making my way to his cock. Finally arriving at my destination. I made love to his perfectly sculpted cock. My mouth sliding up and down with exact harmony to his movement. Taking my Tongue and gently flicking under the head with rapid movements making the gyrations of Elvis on stage. He could not withstand the perfect pressure that I was putting as my head slid up and down his rock hard cock. Finally he said I am going to shoot and keeping my mouth and tongue under his head and pointing the pee hole to his face I worked it over he shot eight stings of cum covering his own face and he could not stop shivering. Finally he rubbed the top of my head and said simply the best I have ever had in my life. I rose up and saw we had an audience of eight other guys watching in aww.

I showered again being totally drenched from my work out on his well maintained body. The lounger next to my partner was open and I rested again. He awoke and said wow we really slept I said well one of us did, I was a bad boy and we laughed and about then the young guy walked by and he said thanks again my partner said you were a bad boy.

The story continues for my partner I was done and just hung out for several more hours why he was still like the energizer bunny. Several more guys got to feel him deep inside and at least three more got the reward of his oral skills. Well, Paris was a success we went back two more times while we stayed in Paris and each time was equally as thrilling.

Taking our rental car we headed to Spain passing some of the most beautiful county I have ever seen. Passing by Barcelona on our way to Sieges Spain. Upon our arrival to Sieges I was exhausted but he wanted to go out I said its too late to go to the bar. Well I quickly found out it was not to late because the bar did not open till eleven pm. What the hell I am normally in bed two hours before the bars even open. We were waiting outside for the bar to open, we went in ordered and started watching the crowd coming in and the more we would look around there were less and less people. I thought they were going to the bathroom and asked him where they all were he told me they were in the dark room that every gay bar had one. So curiosity got the better of me and I said let's go.

We made our way back into what I would describe as a corral style walkway with wooden stalls. I lost track of my partner quickly into the maze of stalls. Each stall had a couple of guys and some had a group of guys very dark but my eyes adjusted and about then I was pulled into a stall and a guy went to his knees and started servicing me. I looked around the stall and heard a noise that I totally recognized my partner had an old fat guy bent over fucking the hell out of him. I told the guy sucking me I did not want to cum yet and pulled out then he crawled under one of the stalls and started sucking a different guy. I kept walking around and saw a hot tall guy, I thought what the hell and pulled my cock out again and he went to his knees and suck me like crazy asked me in Spanish if I would fuck him, I understood because my partner taught me enough Spanish to be dangerous. Told him no I was oral only so he kept sucking me off. I finished in his mouth and he gobbled like a thanksgiving turkey. As he was finishing me an another guy came up behind him pulled his ass up and entered with out even asking. He really started to moan as I finished cumming in the guys mouth the top came quickly and we both had the hottie clean us off. It was a crazy first experience for my first bar in Spain. I went back to the bar knowing I was in for a long night of sitting alone. A younger guy with two friends came in and they stopped next to me speaking Spanish even though I have owned a home in Mexico for over ten years I hadn't learned enough Spanish to carry on a lengthy conversation. Said I was sorry English? Then he started speaking to me in English.

Made me think why are Europeans so adapt to knowing a second and or third language and Americans are so lazy when it comes to learning a language.

He asked me if I were interested in going to the dark room and I said yes. I did not want to tell him that I may not be able to get hard again but I did not want to at least try. So we slowly made the way back our hand in hand to the stalls. He started kissing me I did not kiss back it is not my thing to kiss strangers. But as he nibbled my neck I slowly unzipped him and making my way to the end of his rock hard cock. Not a huge one I would say average but it was perfect to suck. I was able to go all the way down which excited him immensely. I made oral love to him for about fifteen minutes and he said he was ready to blow. I got up and finished nibbling on his neck and jacking him off shooting all over a guy standing next to us.

We made our way back to the bar and his two friends said what the hell we thought you left. He told them in Spanish something and they both gave me a thumbs up. About that time my partner sat down next to me giving me a kiss which was defiantly not wanted, so I introduced them and they all started talking in Spanish leaving me out of the conversation but not out of the topic. I know they were talking about fucking me and my partner said he was the only guy that has ever fucked him and it was staying that way. Not because of him but that's the way I wanted it to be in our relationship.

We took a break the next day and went to the nude beach where were found a cave in the rocks about twenty feet from the waters edge, and slid into it and watched everyone walk by very entertaining spying on people that did not know you were there. He would translate some of the conversation for me if they were interesting. Many ladies walking by with their swinging cock husbands. And some like me more turtle like, or the old saying grower not a shower in my case neither. It was a good day of relaxing and watching the local and tourists mingle together. Always fun to watch the guys look at other guys when their wife is not looking.

That afternoon we found a guy online that wanted both of us to join him in his room on the ocean. We did and had a great time using him several times until we were all exhausted. He provided drinks and what ever we want very nice guy and very willing to provide us both with equal attention which is rare normally one person hits if off more than the other. But since I cum quicker normally I am the one trying to fill my time. And his view of the ocean was a perfect distraction. We asked him what he was doing in town vacation he said no working but his wife was going to join him later and extend the work to a vacation. There was no way anyone would think he was married to a lady. I was wondering how he was getting three loads of cum out of his ass in time for her to join him. But not our worry and we moved on knowing we would not see him because he was about a fifteen minute drive away.

Later that night we did a repeat of the bar seen and basically a repeat of the debauchery in the dark room. But fun was had by all and guys seem very satisfied. The bar was narrow and you could not help but rub someones cock or ass when walking from one end to the other. I accidentally rubbed one guy more than I thought and he grabbed me thinking I did it on purpose. I said sorry in English which started a ten minute conversation and me buying him a drink. Then somehow we ended up in the corral he more than paid me for the drink. And again I ran into my partner well my crotch ran into him he was crouched the walkway sucking a guy. This was fairly common place and he enjoyed it unless it was a young guy trying to but in then it was not so enjoyable. I think we left about three in the morning. How in the hell do these guys get up for work when they literally are getting home when most people are heading to the job.

We decided to take the train the next morning to Barcelona so we thank goodness we took the train because I was still drunk from the night before. From the train station we walk a fairly long walk to the bathhouse it was down a narrow ally honestly very nonde-script building with a sign so small it was totally forgettable. Finally after walking by a couple times found it more due to the number of men walking in more than the sign. Interesting you paid and then went down a set of narrow steps to a locker area. From there went to a fairly nice rooms, dark hallway, x-rated gay movies and then to a large group room. There was no way when you walked in the top at street level you could ever think there was this huge under-ground cavern of mazes, rooms etc. This is the place that my part-ner did Santa Clause. A huge guy with white hair and white beard. Normally he does not like that kind of guy but he said he always wanted to do Santa.

After a week of late night bars, and almost daily trip to Barcelona bathhouses we were heading to Nice' the next morning. My daugh-ter texted and asked if we were ok due to the terrorist attack in France. It was when the people were killed by running them over with a truck. Said no were were still in Spain but heading there this morning. After a bit of research we found out our hotel was directly in front of the area where the massacre of innocent lives were sickly murdered for no reason. So I woke him up and asked what are his thoughts about going. We both decided that it would be best to not go and try and have a good time while so many people were suffering. So as is normal we cancelled our room which the damn assholes still charged us for because they have a no cancellation policy. I am alway amazed about the greed of people and how they talk a good talk but when it comes to them the Bull Shit does not apply.

We drove back to Paris and found a beautiful hotel to spend our last week in Europe. We went to the famous Bear Bar again the last week almost every night. What a great place three levels but most of the people were outside in the street area that was closed off and turned into a pedestrian mall. Inside was a very narrow bar and room maybe could seat a total of twenty people but there was an open stairwell in the front and one narrow one in the back of the room leading to two levels the second level down encircled the one below. The bottom level had an open room all the walls were stone and rock, dark damp and a perfect place for a murder mystery. And then you walk a little farther there were drink rails and a dark cave area which was very active. I was shocked that drinking and sex were such a combination. But once you got someones attention at the bar you just head down the stairs and the next thing you know totally by accident their cock was in your mouth. Yes we were at the bar every night for many reasons.

That trip was one of three and always ended up at the same bar. Quick side story our second trip was two years apart and we were heading to the bar and my partner said I bet the bartended will remember us, I said no fucking way its been two years. We walked in and there were three bartenders and all of a sudden our main guy looked up and yelled how are you and came running around the bar and hugged us both like old friends. As we were drinking our first drink I said how did you know he would remember and he said we are the only ones that Tip!

In London we visited what I considered one of the strangest Bathhouses we had ever been in it looked like at one time it was a train station well at least from the outside but was built into the side of rock but it was in a city location. I did not like it at all huge open room with vending machines and TVs . And two dark hallways very long with steam rooms, that leaked on the floor and made it very slippery. I was glad there were no lights because the slime and nastiness of the floors would have made me run like a kid. Not all bathhouses are clean and pristine and all I wanted to do was leave once we entered. Not a fond memory.

There was another one in a residential area houses on both sides and lined up just like any other neighborhood it was totally unlike the other one. This was two stories with rooms and a walkway on the second story overlooking a glass atrium in the middle. It has a pool and steam room that had a round glass shower in one section and a dark room inside the huge steam room. Lots of action happened in the steam area. My favorite memory was when I was sitting no the edge of the pool and a young guy swam up stood in front of me and proceeded to suck me off in front of about twenty guys. He started something because a few minutes later everyone was fucking or getting sucked around the pool. We all hit the steam room showers at the same time and it started all over again. My partner was with an old guy in a private room and missed all the action. But in honesty they were all young except for me and he would not have enjoyed it. But on the other hand I had a great time.

Since covid has hit we have not been back to Europe can't wait till this is one and we can start having more adventures. As I mentioned there are sex clubs that are only for the true adventurist and I may not partake but I want to see them.

12

LATER IN LIFE

The deeper I get into the lifestyle of the gay community I am shocked how many guys have children. And that meant that I was not as unusual as I once thought. There is a huge percentage of guys that come out later in life. Many of them come out after a divorce which is what happen in my case. And the more I started thinking about this I started my research of the people that I personally know and it comes to about twenty percent. So if twenty percent come out after a divorce how many more are out there that are unknown and still married. But the late in life phenom is the one that I am starting to really think about and the question is why.

Earlier in the book I suggested that this was a craze and getting more and more prevalent in our society. The reason or reasons for the change in personal preference are many and I am sure there are more than I can consider but let's look at a few of them.

1. Females Stop Having Sex
2. Females Stop Wanting Sex
3. They have always been Bi or Gay and just tired of hiding
4. They get caught

5. Wife/Husband Dies
6. Fall in love with a friend
7. Public Opinion has changed
8. Children are grown
9. Parents are both dead
10. Can't find a opposite sex partner
11. Religion
12. Tired of the same person
13. Easier
14. Job/Retirement
15. Disease not so Much

I will try to explain each of these from my perspective. This is obviously not scientific or analyzed from a professional point of view. But if you are like most people all of the mumbo jumbo is not truly reality. Somehow my common since approach is closer that what any professor can embellish on about societal norms and evoluton of humanity, bla bla bla.

1) Females Stop Having Sex

As females age many of them just give up sex the desire is gone and it may be physical or psychological but they just don't enjoy doing it any more. Some I know have a physical change and sex is painful due to dryness etc. That is understandable if it hurts every time how can it be a joy even though your partner still wants it. For no reason apparently I use Females as the example, it can also males in any or most of the scenarios.

2) Females Stop Wanting Sex

And many females I have talked to just get tired of trying to please their partner because it is one sided affair. For years they tried and never felt fulfilled so it is easier to walk away from sex all together than having a demanding partner that can not be satisfied and they shut down. But they shut down in many ways sexually, conversationally, mentally and turn to a different way to satisfy their needs. Much like when a person changes and decides the same sex is what they truly want the same happens in the reverse. Instead of having something different they want nothing at all and there in lies their point of difference.

And after the change in life many people are no longer interested in sex at all. This is one thing that happened to me the longing and desire

3) They have always been Bi or Gay and just tired of hiding

It's not like one day they wake up and say today is the day I confess and move on. But it is a build up over time and the feeling is they cannot hide any longer and whether it is guilt or something else they are done hiding.

4) They get caught

Once we or they get caught coming out or being open to the lifestyle is pretty much a for gone conclusion. But many people have an underlying desire to get caught because they can not confess so getting caught seems easier. To that I say it is wrong because if you are honest you are putting the burden on the partner. And in every way that is fair to the partner. But early on in the book we talked about being prepared and this is the reason because if it happens suddenly you need a plan and surprise is not a plan.

5) Wife/Husband Dies

When a long life partner dies many people do not want the struggle of finding a replacement for that person. They still want sex but they don't want someone to replace the love of their life. And finding a person of the same sex actually enables them to have sex with out the replacement feeling. Many older people feel there is no-one that will ever measure up to their partner so why try. And they turn to the gay or bisexual lifestyle to give them the comfort with out the commitment. This also in a weird way shows their family they are still mourning the loss of their loved one.

6) Fall in love with a friend

This is one of those that is much more common than we can imagine. Their best friend and them go to the gym together golf together see each other in the shower and one thing leads to another and it happens they start playing. At first it is curiosity and that leads to sex and then love. I guess you could say it's their Frankie and Gracie moment.

7) Public Opinion has changed

As things in life change and the acceptance of being gay or bi has grown many people in the older age bracket decide now is the time and begin their open life. So it may not be at all, that they became gay or bi later in life but they just finally announced it and stopped hiding who they truly have become.

8) Children are grown

Many people wait till they are no longer responsible for children to make the move and tell the truth. Once the responsibility is over then we feel free to come out and tell the truth and again due to age that normally happens in our fifties. In the chapter about influences this is one more reason our family influences our outcome and decisions in life. We all gage how we think our kids will handle the truth and if we feel unsure it will take us longer to make the announcement. Only when we feel that we know the outcome of them knowing will we say anything. Most of us are more concerned about Parent and Kids than spouse. I know that may sound cruel but it is reality.

9) Parents are both dead

I am totally convinced that many people that are bi or gay hide it more from their parents than from their spouse. It would be harder for them to tell their parents no matter what age than their spouse at any age. So if people are hanging on to come out it make since that this will happen later in life. I find this in people that are older than 60 typically.

10) Can't find a opposite sex partner

As many of the dozens of dating sites can attest it is hard to find a partner. And even harder to find a partner later in life that is sexually active and not looking for a sugar daddy. Many people that have been successful in life are afraid that people only want them for their money. Those people should never think that there are not just as many of the same sex that are doing the same thing. As a matter of fact I feel that in the gay lifestyle the percentage is higher. Many Younger looking for older is not the fact they like older but they go where the money is and normally that is older not younger.

But finding a partner is hard and a true life partner is harder no matter same or opposite sex. But sex only, is much easier for a guy to find a guy to have sex with than a female. Not that I want all guys to sound like we are whores but many of us are in the gay lifestyle. Many are open to sex period and sometime with a guy we would never want to be with but sex is sex and that over powers all most everything else. Yes I understand this is one opinion and it is not true under all circumstances. But it is very common and should not be ignored as being part of many gay especially males, life.

11) Religion

And for some people religion still plays a part in them being outwardly who they are on the inside. Even though there are many open minded churches today. The old standards more traditional churches still have the believe that homosexuality is a sin. And for that reason you are more apt to not come out especially if you are a believer in the religion. It is one reason why the number of people going to church has declined for decades. Many believers are switching to a different church still believing in God but not the traditional church. And that gives them the openness to be accepted in a place they felt uncomfortable.

12) Tired of the same person

Many times we have just had enough and are done with the marriage no matter what. As you have read here the negativity for me became more than I could stand and just had to walk away. When you are in a relationship that is a constant battle everything becomes a disagreement or you just start giving in because you can't stand the consequences, it is over. And yes sexual preference plays a roll in the outcome of a marriage but it is not in many cases the major factor but it is the underlying factor. When you get tired of years of abuse or fighting or name your poison it is just time to say enough is enough. And most people from certain generations stay longer than others. But people finally give up and that takes years contributing to one more reason there is an influx of guys later in life.

13) Easier

When you spent a lifetime arguing and fighting over sex, not getting enough of it and you see how easy it is to get on the other side you start to think why am I putting myself through this. It is so easy just go get what you want when you want it and there is no fighting, arguing begging its there when you want it and sometimes when you don't. And again it can and does take years and years of putting up without till we find out how much easier it all is not the other side.

14) Job Retirement

After people retire there is no more worrying about company's approval or not. We think we live in a society that it is ok and there is nothing to worry about. But the reality is, there is a judgment that is still going on and will maybe always go on. Yes it is a hundred times better but when we hear others talk is it better or are they just acting like it is better? They say the right things in public but in private their attitude is totally different. You know what I am saying and maybe you are one of those that are not tolerant at all. But if that were true you would not have read the book this far I am totally convinced of that.

15) Disease not so Much

Later in life after guys stop having sex with their wife they are not nearly as concerned about passing on a disease. So in knowing that if they catch something their partner will not nor will they ever know. So we are much more apt to play knowing we can not hurt their health due to our actions.

So all in all there are many reasons that we come out later in life and again I have probably only scratched the surface but I feel these are the main reasons for the later in life homosexual and bi sexual explosion.

STORY 12: MEMPHIS MAN NIGHTS

– XXX –

There is a swingers club in Memphis that once a month one night only it turns into a gay sex club males only. So after finding out about the club I knew I would have to find a way to go. Still married it made it tricky but surprisingly I found a way. Not once but three times. A little different than the normal male female swingers club where you typically have your clothes on, here you could not go to the second floor unless you stripped to underwear or nothing only. As I walked in and paid I was handed a paper bag and a marker to put my name on it and place the clothes, phone etc in the bag and give to the bartender he will staple it shut and keep it safe. I was shocked by the size of the club huge theater screen with many couches spread around. As I continued to walk through familiarizing myself with the layout, I walked through a doorway and there was a maze of sorts, noticed it was a dead-end but dark and narrow. I turned around looking down and saw the unmistakable oval glory holes. I bent over to take a look and simultaneously was hit in the face with a huge black cock. Damn my lucky day! Sucking and making oral love to his joyous manhood till I thought he was going to blow, he pulled out and bent over saying great job but he didn't want to cum yet. Thank goodness because I didn't want to disappoint him with out taking the load in my mouth.

Trying to get out of the narrow passage there were now many guys on their knees sucking cock. Finally got over and around them, to finish checking out the rest of my new favorite place. I rounded the corner and saw the other side of the maze. There were 8 guys with their cocks through the walls and I assumed they there must be 8 more guys on the other side which was fairly accurate based on the space that I just walked through. Everyone was involved in their own fun not paying much attention to anything else, except for one guy that was finger fucking the guy next to him while they both were getting sucked through the glory hole.

Making my way further came to several alcoves with beds chairs, couches and TV's playing gay sex movies. Then accidentally I found a back set of dark stairs that made there way to the second floor. Once arriving there I was greeted with several individual rooms approximately 20 of them some with doors some without then found several large group rooms. Then I happened upon a hall that opened up to a wall of seating and at the end several huge cages. In the one cage was a guy holding the bars begging to suck cock. The other cage there was a guy ass backed up to the bars feet outside getting fucked by three that were taking turns with him.

Heading back I saw a room that I had missed I asked one guy what was in there. He said dark-out play room it was so packed it was all I could do to squeeze in and let the crowd have their way with me. In this room no was not an option if I said no thanks another guy was already taking his place. So I let them grope fondle suck, lick what ever they wanted. Finally making my way around the room to the exit. The next room had a door it was slightly opened and I looked in, two guys were making out and they motioned for me to come in and I did. They continued while I got to my knees and serviced both at the same time. Both Very young 21 maybe with chiseled bodies and impressive rock hard manhood. For being young they were much better at sharing than I thought they would be. I would work on one for a minute he would pull out of my mouth and the other was inserted. Occasionally both would enter my warm moisture filled mouth. About fifteen minutes I felt it was time to move on saying thanks they both kissed a cheek and I left. As I did, I turned around and saw another couple had entered the room one of the young guys went on his knees on the bed getting ready to take a load in his perfectly sculpted ass. So stopping to watch the action for about five minutes and got horny as hell again.

Finally I came to an open area looking down where there were a huge set of steps which was the main stairway that would normally lead to the second level once you leave the bar area behind the movie screen. Then making my way a set of open room four in all but connected with open door frames. And then there she was on a huge leather couch was yes she! And she had just started undressing for a fairly thin black guy. And I overheard a few guys talking about it, not happy she was there.

Quickly found out there were two partners in the business and the wives would just show up with the husband's on gay night. She had several black cocks that she wanted and they only came out on the gay event. As she started getting pounded her husband watched so I started talking to him. I said that it was so hot to see that massive cock pound her. He said yes he loved it, and then he reached down and felt my cock and he said this is more my liking. Going down to his knees and taking my rock into his mouth sucking just a few inches from his wife's face. She said suck it baby! I backed up slightly so others could watch and a couple more guys stood next to me and I started stroking them. I looked down at my sucker and said you want two more. Yes he did so he took turns on the three of us while his wife was starting to get fucked by Big Black Cock number two. I had been so distracted I hadn't notice a different black guy fucking her while she sucked the first one. About a minute later her mouth was full of thick white milk running out of the side of her mouth. So much cum I instinctively grab her husband's head and moved to her and made him lick it off her face. Then back to us. The three of us, almost like it was planned the guy to my right said I am cuming, quickly moved his mouth that direction just in time for the load then I said me too and load shot just before his open mouth was there but he still managed to get it all. As he finally was getting every drop from my cock the last guy unloaded. Another huge load he gagged and she said swallow it you cunt. While making a lot of noise she came again and her new black mate said I am ready to cum she said feed the bitch. He pulled his huge black cock out of her pussy and shoved it in her husbands mouth. And swallowing his fifth load he left for the bathroom and she followed closely behind. He came back from the bathroom and I said thanks and asked why they came out on gay night. He told me that with their normal crowd of customers in the swing club did not know he liked cock. So I said so its not for your wife? No she comes along to give me cover to my cock addiction. And most guys don't mind much especially sense she only fucks the same two guys each time.

I took a break and walked around plopped down on the couch to watch the porn on the big screen projection TV. That break lasted about five minutes when a young guy stood next to me and took out his cock stroking it a few inches away from my mouth. I wasted no time and took it in my mouth he said I am going to fuck you I said no I don't get fucked. Damn man you got a perfect ass and I will make you feel like you have never felt. But the disappoint soon vanished as I started sucking him like no other. He was getting ready to shoot so I looked up at another guy that was watching us and said you want the load. Yes he did and I pulled off and he got there just in time to take several squirts in his mouth. That was my first visit and two more times that I visited it was very much the same except neither of the other times that I visited were the owner and wife were there. Later I found out that the two gay guys that rented the building had asked the owners not to attend because so many guys were upset about it. Well I was not surprised that the guys complained because she got two big cocks, lol. WOW what a great group of people.

13

GIRLFRIEND COVERUP

Many times I find that gays that have not come out and are married will actually take a mistress before taking the next step of being out. Or many or should I say most never come out, they remain closeted bi. This will help them with the coverup and continue the lie even farther, as none of their friends would guess them being gay with a wife and girlfriend. There are several reason for the girlfriend on the side. One is honestly you can get them to do things sexually that you would never ask your wife to do or that your wife will not do. And while that helps you sexually getting closer to fulfillment it is still not there. Now you will juggle a mistress, a wife and your true gay life. This creates extreme mood swings trying to juggle different lives that you are lying about to almost everyone you know. The other item is the assistance of the coverup.

The double or now for some triple life creates stress beyond belief and causes more problems at home than there were. Not only do you have the regular home life normal everyday situations that is compounded by trying to make the girlfriend happy and still find time to take a walk on the wild side with guys. And know one can or should know what you are going through. In this lifestyle you can truly trust no one to keep all your secrets. You may get away with hiding the gay part of your life but most guys for some reason need to brag about having as they say, a piece on the side. But here is a little secret that most people do not know many times when a guy talks about the side action with their friends they say it is with a hot chick but the reality is that the story may be true but it is not a female but a male that they are sharing the interlude stories with.

My long term mistress that actually may have caused my first divorce was very young and willing to do more and teach me more than I ever thought possible. Her appetite for sex was insatiable. The very first time we road to a work event together and in the middle of a dark long stretch of road she without notice or conversation leaned over and started sucking me as I was driving. Well from that point on it was game on every time I had the chance to see her I would. Truly became infatuated with sex and kinky sex with her. Stories about her lesbian affairs would drive me crazy.

I will not say she caused my first divorce but she opened my eyes to the possibilities of what I was missing and created a longing that I had been harboring internally for years. The irony was that she liked the fact that I was married it was her turn on controlling another women's husband. As soon as I told her I was getting divorced she dumped me.

As life would have it I learned a lesson well at least for a few years. The almost twenty years of marriage took two years to get out of with the divorce and more heartache that anyone should endure. The old saying "hell has no furry like a woman scorned", learned the true meaning of the statement. Even to this day over twenty years later it is still hard for my first ex to be nice. As my daughter was growing up never did I say a bad word about her mother even though there was plenty to say. Locking her out of the house in the winter so I would have to drop what I was doing and run and pick her up then blame a young girl for allowing to be locked out. Not buying her cloths or even a winter coat even though she got sizable child support. Every step of the way she would find something to cause stress and heartache. She was totally crazy and obsessed with paying me back her only reason for existence was to make my life miserable. I have to say those were the darkest days in my life not because of me but because of what my daughter had to go through. My first ex knew she could not do anything to me but hurting my daughter was the only control she had left. And the abuse was so bad mentally, but never physical, that my daughter petitioned to live with me and won in the courts. How bad does a mother have to be to loose custody in the 1990's pretty damn bad is all I will say. First of all I take one hundred percent of the Blame it was my fault for the divorce the next many years have passed and I still feel regret and am ashamed of my actions. I should have gotten the divorce because we did not get along and not find or create a reason for the divorce. I still feel it actually brought my daughter closer to me and for that I am grateful. A ray of sunshine from a bitter ending.

I still from time to time think of my ex lover and what would have happen if we had stayed together. She married a very straight acting guy in a word I would call him boring. She has a son now and life seems good for her. I ran into her shortly after her marriage and I had remarried also. We reminisced and I told her I still wanted to be with her she said her too. She asked me if I ever regret us not trying harder to stay together the truth was yes but only because I felt that I could have brought other guys into our life with out the fear of loosing her. Of all the girls I have been with she was the only one that I ever felt to be open to guy on guy sex. Because of her propensity to have and want sex with women it would be an easy sell because she knew why there was such a desire.

STORY 13: THE GIRL FRIEND ADVENTURES

− **XXX** −

She and I had so many interludes and so many chances to do even more that never materialized. We had several times set up rendezvous with another couple where the other girl was bi but it always fell through. The first night we got together was one of the best blow jobs ever, when she came over and starting unzipping me I knew I needed to find a side road not a four lane highway. I pulled off ASAP by that time she already had my raging hard cock in her mouth. I could not find a driveway so I just stopped in the middle of the road. I had to set the seat so I could see if there were any cars coming our way. After she finished I started to drive again. Fuck no she said it was her turn so in the middle of the highway on a dark lonely road between Cedar Rapids and the Quad Cities I again stopped the car, got out and with a stretch of road where we could see for miles I opened her car door she swung her legs out, laid back and I went in between them with a tongue that was almost as hard as my cock had been.

I worked her clit over till she came two times yelling and screaming for me not to stop, I looked up and said shit there is a car coming and all she did was laugh. I jumped in the driver side and took off we both laughed when he truck passed us. If he only knew what we were just doing. The entire way home she was fingering herself and feeding me all her juices. I smelled of sex my hair was wet with her juices my shirt smelled like her. I am not complaining but when I get home I will need to make up an excuse why I did not get into bed and slept in the guest room. I was good at making up lies, I got so good at it that I actually believed the stories myself.

Another time we both were working the same area in Champaign Illinois she was riding in my car. All of a sudden with out warning at a stop light in the middle of the city she came over and starting sucking me with cars on both sides watching. All I could do was sit there because I sure as hell was not going to stop her. We got the the next traffic signal and she looked up at the young guy giving her a thumbs up. With my load all over her face she took her finger and made sure it all went in her mouth as he watched.

At the next light he was on her side and she lifted up he blouse and started licking her nipples. We could see he was jacking off I asked if she wanted to suck him she said no. Thank God! I was not wanting to share her. After the next stop light she pulled down her pants and fingered herself while everyone next to us could see and they all seemed to enjoy the show. She would pull out her fingers and feed me her wet pussy juice. It was hard to top this display of sensuality with anything I ever did since. I was mesmerized by her openness to doing anything. She was the first person to ever tie me up and literally fuck me all night long. I would wake up and she was sucking me four times that night she road me like a dildo that would not stop.

She was the first person to ever put their tongue in my ass hole and thus made me cum with out touching my cock. She worked that tongue like she was trying to lick the last bit of peanut butter from a jar. I was not much of a shooter but that afternoon I shot the load on my face, the only time I have ever cum while being ass eaten. I yelled OMG, I am going to cum her tongue got deeper and faster. She looked up saw all the cum and slowly moved up licking all the cum off me. She took my limp cock in her mouth and worked it over till I was rock hard again. She brought up her wet pussy had me lick it to assure total saturation and slid down and fucked me. Telling me she want my cock in her virgin ass. I tried but could not enter the tight hole.

One day we were again working the same area and met up and went to a state park and up on a ridge over looking the highway we fucked while people were walking the trails next to us. We got done and she wanted more we made it to the car and I was on my knees outside her door licking her pussy till she got so noisy I was embarrassed and had to stop. She was pissed, she had no filter and did not care who saw us.

But no matter what when I was working areas and she was not around to keep me on the straight and narrow (if we can call what we did straight and narrow) I would find my way to a porn cinema and there would always be several cocks in my mouth. No matter what I still had the desire to be with the same sex.

So at that point in my life I started to think that no matter how much sex I was getting I still needed and desired male on male action. I could not live life without another male to have sex with, and not just one male it have to be different men.

14

THE TRANSITION FROM BI TO GAY TO BI

You would think after getting this far in the book I would know if I am bi or gay. I don't, but I also don't care. For god sake if I were talking about going through a transition and making a surgical decision then it may matter because that is a great psychological strain on the mind and soul. But when people meet me there is no way that they would know one way or the other if I were bi, gay or straight. And I honestly like to keep it that way because the facts are they don't think about it at all, so why should I spend time or energy dealing with things that are not important to anyone.

I truly know that I have always been bi but then there was a number of years that it was only men and now for the past several years I have gotten back into the couples when possible. Where pleasing a lady orally brings me great satisfaction. And watching the two of them interact is of great fantasy for me. Every couple is entirely different and what brings the excitement of the great unknown when we first meet.

With some couples the guy only watches and does not participate at all he is a real chuck. But most are right in the middle of it while I am on her, he is having her service him and vice versa. There are so many guys that love having me take care of her and he finishes her orally. Every couple is different and that is what makes it exciting. They seem to have great relationships because they know what they want and they go for it with out hesitation.

I am hoping to have that one day, where I can reach the point being totally at peace. So asking the question if I am bi or gay maybe not be the real question but am I comfortable in Being.

Being who we are, nothing more or less is truly reaching a peaceful life. Sometimes we put the importance of sex above all other and the real life is sex should be an extension of our life not the reason for our life. And growing is all part of it once we feel we reach an end but we never get to the end except in death. So changing and moving to the place getting us closer to our goal knowing that we will never reach it.

Let's hope that we all will find our place in life that we are at peace in our own skin. And if we could all only reach that place then all the world troubles would be gone. I will say now that in my past I would listen to people that I totally find unappealing and agree or laugh along even though I totally disagree with their statement. Because I wanted to fit in I said nothing well those days are over. While I am not going out of my way to create a problem or ever be rude but letting people know that it is no longer acceptable to say things about other people that are different. But when someone tells a joke I am also not so closed minded or offended if someone is just being themselves. I have said that being thin skinned with no since of humor is just as dangerous as a small mind.

As a society we don't agree with everyone but we ALL need to take time to listen. Understanding is the new goal for all of us if we only realize it before it is too late and we are so divided. Let's come together, let's understand, let's truly love one another for or differences and be accepting of people no matter what. It will take one person to start let that one person be you.

So in summing up the topic of this chapter Gay or Bi or what ever does not make the person the person makes the person.

STORY 14: MY HOTEL PARTIES

– **XXX** –

placed an ad on Squirt for a sex party in my hotel room for the following night in Iowa City. I always wanted to do this but was nervous as hell being the first time. I would get emails with pictures from each potential party participant. And trying answer the endless questions from several guys was exhausting. One guy almost hourly ask how many are coming. The big night arrived I checked into the Marriott and sent out the room number to a dozen guys. At 7 there was a knock and another and another finally 8 guys were there within a few minutes. Several knew each other and that made it better. So I said what are you all waiting for and that's all it took. Everyone was undressed and formed little groups and they were off to the races.

The group was a mix of college guys to a retired professors. My two bedroom suite was too big to see all the action all the time due to the separate room but I defiantly was addicted to the Group Parties. One thing about the parties was how open the married men were and they felt sexually liberated. I wondered after the party if the married guys tried seeing if their wife's were more open to different forms of sex. For me it became more of what I was missing in my sex life and I knew that the subject was off limits after getting shot down once the adventure of the sex clubs had passed.

If they were a bottom there was always a willing cock to fill them. Somehow and to this day cannot figure out how without saying a word guys know if the other one is a bottom. Since I am not a very good top and do not have a lot of practice at it, my knowledge base is limited. There was a young blond he was the nights sub if someone wanted a special thing done he provided the mouth, ass, tongue etc. To say he was the cum dump would be accurate when guys were ready to cum he would finish off each and every one, many more than two times. He actually made it known to everyone what he wanted and more accurately needed as much cum as he could get during the night. There was one moment when a guy was cumming by making a lot of noise and he ran over and said feed me the guy said sorry I just shot in his ass as soon as he pulled out he was sucking the cum out of the others hole. Defiantly not my cup of tea but everyone has their own thing just not me.

It was getting near the end and one guy left so I opened the door to let him out and guy was standing outside the door as I opened it, I welcomed him in he sat on the bed and looked around. So hot that we all were looking at him, thinking he was just shy, I got between his legs unzipped and went down on him. What a beautiful cock, the nicest one I had that night. I could tell he was getting ready to shoot so I motioned for blondie and he took it like a trooper gaging but not spilling a drop.

The guy said he had to go, ok I said asking him if he were on the list said no he was on the way to get his wife ice and heard the noise. Sure enough there was an ice bucket outside my door. Then he said I will tell her I went to lobby and a guy from work stopped me. So I guess we never know how our first time will be with another guy but he did tell me that was his first time but now not his last. Jokingly I said "Fuck her good" he said "well now I will get rock hard just thinking of this moment". The rest of the guys were in shock when I relayed the conversation. They started to drift out the door telling what a great time they had. I agreed and blondie was the last to leave not without eating my ass and swallowing my last load I could muster up for him. I sleep like a baby the next morning found underwear that was not mine wondering who forgot to put it on.

15

NO BETTER NO WORSE

In being gay, bi or straight or undecided you are no better or no worse that anyone else. I am shocked that somehow we celebrate being gay, Why? Why do people feel that somehow that is worthy of praise and pats on the back. If gay people want to feel a part of everything stop thinking some how you are special you are not, you just are. We as gay or bi or trans or name your gender when we stop looking for attention then and only then will you be equal. You strive for equality but the more you say people look at me funny or talk behind my back and then you make a big deal of it you are only creating the division you say you don't want. So are you really just trying to attract attention? Look deep and long at your self you will find the real answer so be as honest as you want everyone else to strive. The world will always have its idiots the minute we give them acknowledgment then they got what they wanted. This is true for both sides of the equation.

Because we feel they somehow have a voice, and by confronting them we give them the voice they desire. And yes it is hard to walk away and say nothing but it is the only way to silents them because once we are not there then they have no voice. And if no one hears them then where is their voice it does not exist.

So in society we are all truly no better or no worse than anyone else. We need nothing special except to be who we are and nothing more. It is why I oppose most groups with a single minded social agenda. Any single social agenda is actually discrimination and when that happens I can not support it. Think about and think hard what that means and see with a totally open mind if I am right. You can pick the agenda and I can be a voice of reason to show how others can and do perceive your agenda.

I understand that this goes totally against what we think we need to do but reality is it is the best way to grow and be as accepting as we all should be. Because if we are not accepting of idiots, bigots, racist how can we rise above to be what we aspire to be. Be it Bi, Gay, Trans, Queer or Straight we are all here and need to truly co-exist not just be a bumper sticker.

STORY 15: BI HOUSE PARTIES

– **XXX** –

As a host of Bi House Parties the stories are amazing and endless. The size of a house party depends on so many things but saying typically we will have 10-20 people. Many people are surprised that the average age is 50+. The other thing about straight swingers is that the husband in many cases is much more bi that the wife knows. In my experience almost 50% of the men would consider either sucking or being sucked by a guy. The stigma is still there even if the females are open to being with a same sex partner the taboo of men on men is still there for no apparent reason. The gay phobia is alive and well with no end in sight. When you go to a bi party you will find everyone friendly and very inclusive but that does not mean you can do anything to anyone. Everyone has limits and likes and dislikes this is not a lifestyle that is for the thin skinned. Be nice and treat everyone with respect and caring. A open sexual lifestyle is not a reason to be a jerk or pushy in any way. Let it flow and never assume.

As I talked about in early chapters and stories when I host my bi parties I took all the lessons of what I experienced and the good and hopefully eliminated the things that people do not like. The first thing is to let people know that no means no and if they are pushy they will not be invited back. Normally this ends all the problems but horny guys sometimes can't help themselves.

She walked in long blond hair beautiful high sitting tits huge by most peoples standards and a mesmerizing face, smile and eyes. She was reminiscent of a nineteen forties black and white move star. I asked her name so we could mark it off because I did not remember any single ladies on the list she informed me that her husband was parking the car. Great your name? And then he walked in equally as stunning as his wife a man that could only be described as breath taking no matter if you are gay or straight he was a beautiful man. He was wearing tight leather pants that left nothing to the imagination so tight I could honestly see the veins in his cock. And what a massive one it was well at least from what I could see so far. This was one of the times that I really wish I were a guest and not the host. Because as a host the policy is not to partake of the beauties unless they spend the night. And after the closing time of the event then I feel it is ok to play.

The unexpected happens every so often and this night was maybe one of the biggest surprises ever. The guest started to filter in and the the cocktail hour was pleasant with great conversations. The hot couple seemed like they were truly making friends and the first activity started with two wives making out and the one laying back on the couch while her friend ate the hell out of her pussy and ass. I was mesmerized by them and hardly noticed the one husband was on his knees sucking the other one.

Someone said let's go on the bed and they all four ventured into the bedroom where two or three people followed. The next thing was the surprising moment of the evening the Hot couple like a switch being turned on the wife became a fucking dominatrices. She made him pull the leather pants down showing his massive cock, forced him to his knees and his cock hung down and touched the floor. And then being ever so forceful asked each guy to slap him as hard as they wanted with there cock did not matter if it were hard or soft. And they were free to use him as they wanted, due to his beautiful body and face every guy took a turn and while the guys were abusing him the wives were on the ground one eating his ass and the other sucking and chewing on his cock.

This went on and in just a few minutes everyone was naked and basically in three big groups the seven in the bedroom and two groups of five or six in the living room the numbers would vary people would move from group to group. They were truly being everything they wanted to be. One single guy with a cock almost as big as the Hottie was lifting his ass up and got under him on the floor and slid his massive cock in and started pounding him he was starting to cry out harder make me yours, his wife looked up from the pussy she was abusing with her tongue and said making him your fucking bitch he certainly is mine. The pounding was relentless and non stop one other husband was getting it from one of the ladies with a strap-on.

The guy was getting close to pounding the cum out of his cock into the Hotties ass and the wife looked up again and said cum in the whores mouth. So he quickly pulled out and shoved the cock from his ass into his mouth and with in seconds he started shooting so much it ran out of his mouth and some hit the floor. Suddenly the wife got up and grabbed his head and said I told you never spill a drop and grabbed his hair and forced him to lick up off the floor. Saying never again cunt you will swallow faster. Yes mam,

So in the first hour everyone had cum including the everyone of the ladies. They were all chit chatting again laying on the floor exhausted. And one of the other wives from the bedroom was staring at the hotties cock so directly his wife walked over whispered in her ear and with out hesitation she was sucking his cock eating it like she had been starving for cock even though she had just finished in the other room. It was just minutes before she had one in her ass and one in her mouth in the bedroom with another wives tongue on her clit. But when you see something like his manhood you have to take it when you can.

Her sucking got everyone started again and within minutes over twenty people were in the living room doing what ever they wanted to whom they wanted. It was one of the best groups that were ever hosted and still my favorite. It does not always work out as well as this group did but what a memory. The hot couple were relaxing a few hours later laying on the couch and I asked if they would like to spent the night so they did not have to drive. And they said that would be great and asked where they would sleep. I said I would change the sheets in the extra bedroom or they could sleep with me. They choose option two, while everyone was saying good by and kissing good bye like I thought the party was going to start again. The wife left took a shower and the hottie hubby and I were talking. I asked if he was ready to shower and he said if I would join him. I did and what a wonderful shower it was I made sure to clean him inside and out.

We made our way to the bedroom where his wife was entertaining her self with one of my huge dildos. He and I crawled in and I moved the dildo and started eating her he was eating my ass and then we switched and I took his huge cock in my mouth and fell in love they were kissing like high school kids under the bleachers. I would move from his cock to her pussy. I was so hard raising his leg and placing my tongue in his ass getting him wet moved up and placed my cock in him while I was kissing her and she moved down and started sucking his huge member. We made love and it was so wonderful she had none of the dominatrices that was present early she was gentle and sensual it was truly making love. I was ready to cum and she whispered please cum in is tight ass for me. About thirty seconds later I did as requested. She was now between the two of us holding us both not wanting to ever let go. We all drifted off to sleep and truly one of the best nights sleep of my life. Woke early in the morning and they said they had to get going but not before they both shared my cock in the most memorable oral releases I can ever remember. While they sucked I asked him to move so my mouth could reach his cock and I gently sucked it not to make him cum just to make him happy. What a Day and what a night.

I have dozens of other stories but this one is the best and they are one of the nicest couples I have ever been with truly memorable.

16

GETTING READY FOR WHAT'S TO COME

As I talked earlier on in the book about my father and his openness to blacks, minorities and less fortunate did not tell the whole story but here is a bit of inside about how I was raised. My mother and father were the kindest gentlest people that I have ever known not to say there were without faults because to be human is to have faults and issues but when I hear people say you are only a stranger once that was how they lived.

We lived in a trailer barely able to get the things we wanted or needed but that did not stop my dad. He was the first to bring home a family or help out a family that was moving from the south to work in the industrial revolution that was still going on in the north. Most of the good paying factory jobs were in the north so the migration was alive and well in my early years. So dad who was an avid CB guy (citizens Band Radio operator) would find people that needed help and bring them home. I was never sure when I got home from school who would be sitting in the dining room table and where I was going to sleep incase dad had the great ideas of having them stay with us until they found a place. Not only did I feel that he was crazy for doing this I felt he actually went looking for these people.

Many years later I came to understand that it was just him. That he truly knew no other way than to be kind to others. Ellen always closed her show by saying "Be Kind To One Another " that was my dad every day. We had nothing, but he was willing to give it away to people that had less. I am always amused by the real racist, the real bashers, there real haters in this world are the ones that protest too much if you disagree with them. Such as when Ellen took flack from the WOKE for sitting with Former President Bush at a baseball game, omg the sky was falling these are the same people that have Zero tolerance for anyone that sees the world in a different light than they do. These are the people that destroy property and want change. What kind of change do they want they don't want change they want conformity they want the world to think like them and then after that when everyone is embarrassed for falling in line with the demanding of the world. People are shocked they do everything they ask then they are not satisfied they will want more.

These are the people that embarrass gays like me and then stab you in the back at first chance because they say the words but deep inside have more HATE than anyone they are talking about. As a nation we have to rise up and let our voices be heard, we can be kind, we can care, we can stop the violence again everyone. But never with violence or protesting in the streets because when we take a stand that takes a march we have lost. We can do it one person at a time just open you hearts and doors and let the good in each other shine through no longer can we teach our children they are victims we should demand more. Go out and earn more be someone that truly cares be my father.

Guys will admit to having an affair with another woman long before they admit to having an affair with a guy. Case in point is me. I never told my ex I was with a guy she assumed it was a woman for a long time. So you wonder how the first few paragraphs fit into this topic. I want to start a revolution one where we all start to understand we all have differences and that is what makes us unique. NOW is the time to stop being scared of who you are and what you are but if you ever put someone down then you are no better. I cringe at every racist, at every skinhead I see, every gay hating jerk but if I act like them I am no different. Getting ready for what's to come is liberating If we all stick together and let people be what they are then ther will be more of us the less of the crazy jerks in the world. And every time we convert one person to being a better person will be one less of them to spread hate.

But at the same time we have to stop spreading hate in or with the disguise of a mask some how we are better. We are not and understanding that will heal us all faster and more honest than anything we can do as a society. Part of our societal healing is sexual almost every person in the world somehow puts sex on a pedestal and wants and needs it from time to time. Some put it just a little higher on the pedestal than most of us.

How does your sexual preference change you? Or should I ask does your sexual preference change you? The answer is simple it should not change you at all. Being true to yourself is who you are. I truly feel that most people that don't like gay people don't dislike them because they are gay but because of the way they act. And we have to agree that sometimes we are over the edge when we say that no one should tell us how to act in our own beds. Totally agree but when we bring our bedroom to the streets who has taken it too far? So it's not the gay that they don't like but it's the acts of some of the gay people. Even I see somethings that I don't want my grandchildren to see.

I am in no way saying that you hide who you are but I am saying you should have personal discretion. There is a time and place for everything and if I want to make out with my boy friend and I do it inside a gay bar no one notices but in church then that may be a different story. I think you get my point if there is a reason why you feel different truly take a deep dive into your way of thinking does anyone need to see your private life?

Not in any way saying you go into the closet but we have to be adults. And as we all grow and mature as a society we want more and that more sometimes will mean we have accepted all aspects of living. One more way that more and more people are moving to the bi side of their sexuality. We are growing into ourselves and being bi or gay may be who we were meant to be long ago. I really feel the everyone needs to get ready because your next stage of life will not be what you imagined it would be just ten years ago.

We are becoming more open in our thinking and as we are it will make us more adventures and sexually we will cross lines that we never thought possible. We will find out that sex is sex, love is love and we don't need one to have the other. As I sit here at South Press a coffee shop in south Knoxville owned by a lovely trans person on the music is "The Times They Are a Changin' by Bob Dylan" for a song written almost sixty years ago it is still a work in progress. And yes its ok we are changin and when the song was written it was about racial equality and today its about justice.

STORY 16: "TO MANY TO TELL" AND WHERE TO FIND THEM ON THE DL

– XXX –

As embarrassment goes this XXX rated section may be my most. You have for fifteen chapters had a story at the end of each that tells of an event or group of events that I felt deserved to be told because they were a progression of my personal transition through life or more correctly my sex life and all its changes. The stories were not told in chronological order. I did not tell of the one night stands, the quick in and out of the porn place the dropping by on my way home and knock one off and only be late by ten minutes. But there are hundreds and hundreds of those stories and every week I could add to them.

I talked to my "partner" last night and in one day in Phoenix he did thirteen guys fucked four and sucked twelve of them. Not sure why he did not suck the one guy (laugh out loud). So when I talk about embarrassments I have never done that many in a single day but very close say 9-10 yes. Once guys are in an environment where everyone is doing what they want and not one person is saying no, why stop. There was one time at the bathhouse in Puerto Vallarta where I was in the dark room on my knees sucking a guy, he was joined by another then another and one more added to the group so I was doing four guys at the same time yes I love group sex. They

were all younger hispanic guys that were having a good time thinking they were using me but the truth is I wanted it more than they.

The same has been true at the bi swingers club not uncommon
to have three or four in a row. The reason we go to the clubs, the
porn places etc is not for the movies but the action. As I said earlier
if your partner said they went in to pick up condoms or whatever,
they forgot the part of going in the back and either dropping their
pants or to their knees before coming home to you. I am not sure if
you can call this an addiction but damn close to it and as many will
see it a mental illness. But honestly a form of enjoyment that many
people totally submit to and if not for society as we talked before it
would be much bigger part of society than it is currently.

The number is irrelevant at this point in life because there is
no way to ever count how many guys and couples I have been with
in the past. But I can tell you every lady I have been with, there is
some irony. The only true count is when I met my "Partner" after
filing for divorce in three months we did it over five hundred times.
I only know that number because it was never less than five times a
day and never more than eight times a day. Yes those are real numbers. In three months we had made love more than in total of my
over thirty five years of the two marriages combined. And there in
lies the problem with sex in the traditional marriage.

It would not be uncommon for me or any Anonymous to drop
by porn stores, put out ads in online hookup sites to have several
sessions before going home.

I was thinking as part of the book is being used to help people
understand if their partner is cheating on them. And one other way
to help you find out is to give you a list of many of the sites guys use
to hookup. Here are a few online hookup sites that you may look
for as you are trying to find out if your partner is having Anonymous

affairs. The list is not complete because the book would be an extra twenty pages but these are many of the most commonly used. Many of them are fee based and the charge will come on the credit card under a marketing or other ambiguous name.

squirt.org
Grindr Ap
Growlr Ap
Manhunt Ap
men4sexnow.com
silverdaddies.com
A4A Ap or Adam4Adam.com
SLS.com SwingersLifeStyle
BLK Ap
Tinder Ap
Jack'd Ap
Surge Ap
Scruff Ap
Daddyhunt Ap
Kinky Ap
Hornet Ap
Romeo Ap
Bicupid ap
Taimi Ap
Ashley Madison Ap
Kiki Ap
freshdudes.com

As you can see that most all of these are for guys and I have not included the normal dating sites some guys use them but not many.

Those sites and many of these are fee based and normally would show up on a credit card bill. So the fee based ones are very scary for Anonymous because they can be traced. Which makes them off limits for general Anonymous hookups, but not totally. Some guys just don't care because they handle the bills and are sure you will never look at the statement. Remember these are typically yearly billings so they only show up once a year another reason why many guys don't think you will ever find the statement.

So it is not a stretch to assume if a person is looking for a hookup they will find one in a very short amount of time. Some of the apps have a Now button that lets them know you are available for the next few hours. When you are a looker or a poster it is fast easy and perfect for the quick hookup. Hardly a day goes by where I don't check my messages on about ten different sites. And once one catches my attention I will start a conversation. One tip is if a guy goes on and on with questions they are not really interested in getting together they are lonely and just want to chat with someone. Most of us are looking for a ready willing and able person to play. And if it is on the DL (down low, which is code for married and playing with out my partners knowledge) the last thing we want is someone that will take time to get to play with.

Most Anonymous are on the DL especially in book stores and porn cinemas. Out of habit I will glance at the ring finger to see what I am dealing with and always shocked when in talking with the guys how open they are to tell they are married or not. In the olden days when you asked if they were married it was obvious to a woman but today there are a ton of gay cheaters. I have gone into several bathrooms of bars, nightclubs etc and found guys sucking each other while their partner is out there without a clue. Even saw a huge brawl once when a guy came out of the bathroom with cum dripping off his chin and his partner went crazy.

Many of the .com have apps and most of the apps have websites. As we talked about in the early chapter if you find that cookies are eliminated and that the history on phone and computers has been erased there is a great chance that your partner is cheating. It may not be with the same sex but cheating non the less.

17

DRAMA DRAMA DRAMA

Drawing near the conclusion of the book has made me think about the suffering that comes with all that has been discussed and how much pain and suffering will sure to follow. Each of you that have read the book have a different reason and perspective. It is one reason that I have had about ten working titles and cannot be sure that I picked the right one. I wanted the title to tell you what the book is about but not so much that if you were seen reading it you would be questioned about it. So intently leaving the second part of the title for the inside and not on the cover. "Anonymous" is a mystery sounding title but when you add subtitle "How to Spot the Other Woman when it is not a Woman". It does bring a much more mysterious meaning to the book and tells what the story is about. "How to Spot the Other Woman when it is not a Woman" tells you that if you are curious about your partner having an affair the guideline of what to look for.

As I wrote about almost everything is the same, it holds true for male-female, male-male, female-female or gender?-gender?. You can make the book fit any scenario that is in your household.

Drama is sure to follow no mater how you want to avoid it, denial will happen in most cases until you have hard evidence that what you suspect is factually accurate. As for the denial you may have real arguments and real proof but it is in our DNA to still deny that anything is going on. The more level headed you are hopefully the more level headed the argument will be and the easier it will be. This brings me to acceptance I recommend that you have your plan done before bringing up the possible affair. If you jump in to the argument without knowing what you are going to do if it all goes south you are setting yourself up for more Drama. As in everything you do have a game plan and follow it. This may take months of planning and the more your suspicions are true the better the plan must be.

Maybe setting money aside quietly so you have a nest egg if the shit truly hits the fan. Having a backup place to stay just incase. Having the total layout of how you are going to get to the truth. The bigger the hole you give your partner the chance to lie the harder it is to get to a conclusion. Because they have spent a long time telling you a lie and you have to unravel the lie piece by piece. This will make the drama deeper and harder to get the possible outcome you want.

In prior chapter I said you must know what you are going to do can you deal with it or not. Remember you will need two outcomes ready because many times the discussion takes a turn that you could never ever consider happening. Be ready for it try to consider every possible scenario and have your plan. If this happens then I will do this but if you go into the discussion in anger there will be only one conclusion the one that you give as an ultimatum. And everything will be lost once drama drama drama is the outcome of any discussion. A few ideas concerning the outcome is the situation is more than you can handle.

Research and know exactly what you owe and your balances

in bank, credit cards, personal loans, what are you responsible for and is there anything that is only in your partners name and you are not responsible for. Know every balance on everything you can find and have it all nice and neat in an organized balance sheet. The more you can do this the faster you can come to the end result. Don't be greedy the law does not give you more because you think you deserve. The more rational you are the faster you can get to the conclusion and the more reasonable you are the more you will get in the long run. Once you start fighting over everything if you decide it is over the only person that wins are the attorneys. Both of my divorces ended in a mess and I thought I was being reasonable but they did not think so and it took years for both. And almost everything I offered to both of them was what ended up happening. Because they were so unreasonable the court sided for the more level fare conclusion. But it still took time and a ton of money.

Giving the example of what I offered my ex that I still own half of a house with in Puerto Vallarta Mexico. I offered her to by my half of six hundred thousand dollar house for one hundred thousand dollars. She turned it down because she thought I was up to something. The truth is I felt guilty and just wanted out but now I am getting half when the house sells so I increased my future by several hundred thousand dollars. So when you are set and know all the facts from a financial view point you may find the first offer is the best offer holding out for more is adding to the drama. Holding out for punishment only adds to your stress and unhappiness.

You will have to remain calm and collective because anything other that compassion and understanding will lead to an unsatisfactory conclusion. I know and understand how hard this will be watching your entire life change in the matter of minutes. Well the truth is your life changed a long time ago but you were unaware of the change. And being the last to know is embarrassing and makes us all resentful. But that will never help you get to the conclusion that you desire.

And now that you have a game plan and have decided that you have covered all the bases and the possible outcomes. It is time for the confrontation and layout your concerns and believes of what is going on. As hard as it is going to be remain calm discuss the options and see what happens. If you decided to stay then this will be long and drawn out showing your understanding and hopefully your mate will do the same. Remember ninety five percent of the time they will still deny and try to have an explanation of what you feel or know. Don't be surprised by the denial you know it is coming so calmly let them know that you knew they were going to deny it but lets just be adults and tell the truth. At this point you will have to lay out the facts and you will hear more denials but stand your ground firmly but with compassion. As we have discussed they truly can not help what is going on in their life and as hard as we all think they are doing it to hurt everyone around them that is not the fact in most cases. It is part of their life that is going on and they have very little control of how it started and how it will end.

I do not have all the answers that may go without saying but likewise I do not have all the questions. Every person has a different set of circumstances and each is unique to them and their partner. But I do know the old saying you catch more flies with honey than vinegar holds true here also.

STORY 17: "SUBS AND DESIRES"

–XXX–

There is an underlying group of men and women that love to be used and degraded. As you have heard from several stories in the book so far about husbands that love to be humiliated by their spouse. There is always a group of guys that even though they are married they love to be subs to other guys.

There is truly nothing they will not do and some of extreme to the point of unsafe and scary. There are guys that will take on as many guys in one night as they can get to cum inside them. I have talked to several that have done over fifty guys in one night where the endless number of guys are pounding them over and over where they strap into a sling and are there for the taking. I have never participated in that but have watch and truly remarkable. At a bathhouse in Chicago I was there for eight hours and a guy never got out of the sling. The entire time he would let man after man fill him with their cock and leave their seed in him. Big or small he took them all and did not want to stop. Guys would fist him up to the elbow and he said nothing. This activity to me is over the top but maybe to them it is normal. I had one sub in a bathhouse in Fort Lauderdale I was walking by the rooms and there was a guy on his knees in the dark. I walked in and he never looked up just begged me to use his toy on him. So I lifted up the pillow and under it was the biggest dildo I have ever seen. It was much bigger than my arm and I said I would try so he got on the bed and put it in the air and begged me to put it in him I did as asked pushed and pushed and finally got the huge head in the hole. With everything I had I pushed till it was in him at least ten inches with another ten to go. Finally I got about fifteen inches in him and it was so big around I had no idea how it fit. I noticed he had a ring on is left hand and asked are you married to a lady. He said yes, but she will not let me be myself. And that says it all in a nut shell people go to extreme when they are not getting what they want. Later I saw him in the group room taking everyone that wanted into his gaping hole.

Sub have a true desire to please, nothing is off limits if their Master wants it. I love the roll playing of having what I want when I want it considering myself vanilla compared to many. Some are way too extreme for me. And in saying they will do what ever a guys asks for is not an over statement. I have seen subs used as a foot stool all night during a party he was on his knees with guys sitting and using his back as a foot rest. It is not aways about sex it is about the humiliation and degrading of them, they love being treated like an object and not a human. One of the guys in a hotel in Chicago was a major and I mean major executive married with grandkids and he came in my hotel undressed and put on a dog collar and for hours was led around the hotel party on his knees by the leach and told to do whatever any of the guys wanted. Afterward he was the last to leave and we sat and talked in his five thousand dollar suite. Said he had so much stress in his life it's the only time he can not worry about business. When he is being made to do things he did not want to do he does not have to think. I went down the elevator and walked him out where there was a very very expensive car there with his own personal chauffeur waiting for him. Handed me a magazine and said stay in touch. He was on the cover!

Since the internet it has become easier and easier to find guys and with that the Sub has been reborn because people can start a conversation and tell deep dark secrets without the other person ever seeing them. The secrets take on a life where fantasy that starts out as a conversation now becomes reality because even if the person never did what they said once they meet it becomes reality. Many times they do it not because they wanted to but because they lied about loving it.

Over all hooking up with all kinds of guys becomes easier also more abundant due to the internet. The number of married guys that no longer have to go to a porn store and take the chance of getting caught being seen has created an even bigger down-low sex desire. They no longer have to sneak in a time to run to the store they are meeting up in the car giving or getting what they want and back home in thirty minutes. I would say that it is so easy now a bigger percentage of guys are partaking as never before. Just last week at Home Depot I noticed a guy with his wife he was looking at me so I looked back and with a nod of the head and heard him telling his wife he had to go to the bathroom we met there. He took out his big dick next to me at the stall and stroked it for a minute till the door opened. I left and a few minutes later he walked passed me and casually gave me his number.

I had seen him before on two gay hookup sites. The guys are getting more and more bold putting their pictures on the sites. I texted him a simple nice to meet you message so if wife saw it he could explain it away. We met and I had no idea he was a total sub. He owned a construction company and again needed someone to control him for an hour. His wife looked like a controlling bitch but that is not the control he desired. I am sure she was totally boring in the bedroom. And with his huge swinging dick I was also sure he had, had many affairs with ladies. But the thing about a guy on guy fling we are not getting pregnant and we do not care who he does because we for the most part are not looking for a relationship we only want sex.

As I talked about early on in the book Love and Sex are not the same. If anything guys cheating with another guy is much easier because there normally is a total lack of commitment. And as most people know guys hate commitment. So in closing this section Subs are pleasing, they do not want to make any decisions. They want total control to go to the Master and the ones who use them. And sex is the best way to give up control for a short period of time.

18

KINDNESS

I have captured many times the word Kindness in the book and with Kindness comes understanding and with understanding comes acceptance. Now, not tomorrow is time for all of us to take the time to search our soul and see if we are what we think we are. Are we just saying the words because someone else said them, and it's the hip thing to say? Do you feel that you are trying to fit in and sometimes say things you truly do not believe? But it is easier to agree then create an issue and have people dislike you. The mob mentality is prevalent in the gay community the group think is alive and well in a community that is full of independent thinkers.

Independent thinking in the gay community is dead and gone. I know people that could no longer go to a bar due to threats from the unlighted. I personally have so called friends not talk to me any longer because I dare challenge a them in a factually conversation. Please don't let the facts cloud my opinion is what I say about them.

If you have ever stopped liking or being friendly with someone based on their belief then ask yourself who is the problem is it really you? When I started this book I said that it is all about the truth, that will not change I am telling everything what the gay community has become is just continuation of the truth. When a bumpersticker is on a car that says "Coexist", we can only hope they mean it. In my experiences people jump in with both feet and just can't bring themselves to the reality they are wrong. When President Trump was in office never has one person be so chastised and he was his own worst enemy. He was never smart enough not to take the bate. He felt he had to defend himself which only created more hatred for him. I felt and still do somedays he was an embarrassment but other days I proud of how he stood up for the country.

Torn between tweets that drove me crazy but knowing deep in his heart he cared for all the people of the country. Never had it been so hard I could defend his policies especially now that everything he did that worked has been undone and the mess is undeniable. The only reason it was done was because he (Trump) did it even if it worked they somehow had to change it into the biggest mess of my lifetime. The part of me that wanted to go back and be Anonymous as a supporter of many of his policies. The truth is never should I hide again and that includes sexually, politically and religiously the three third rails of socially getting along.

Don't hide no matter what, if you believe it, have your beliefs with class and understand that as long as you are kind and understanding you can't hold peoples hate for you and with your opinion is the fault of society. They are almost made to be the way they are because they are trying to fit in to a box they have chosen to be placed. One on one you may be much closer than you ever thought you could be. But there are some real diehards that will never see anyone else point of view as credible, no matter the facts. I hope that I will never become so jaded in life.

And if you choose in life to remain Anonymous that's ok also because every person has the knowledge of their own personal limits and if you are not ready now or you are never ready to stop being Anonymous that's your choice.

You can be Anonymous or you can be real I am not here to tell you which is best for you but Anonymous is fun but not real. Eventually you will have to find yourself and when you do I sincerely hope you are brave enough to see your true image not the one you hope you see.

STORY 18: "CROSS DRESSERS"

– XXX –

I am meeting more and more guys that want to crossdress most of them are married to women but can not live their fantasy with their wives. Here are a few stories that I am living at the current moment.

I have a thirty year old married Sub that loves to dress as a girl or woman. He has realistic tits that look and feel like the real thing. He will dress in a school girl short skirt and and a tied top showing off the huge tits. At first I was not really liking the look but now I truly enjoy the play time.

He drops over on the way to work gets dressed and makes sure that I am taken care of in any way that I desire. He calls his ass his pussy and his cock his clit. He loves the use of huge dildos in his pussy then after I have stretched him out I put my cock in his pussy and unload mostly in him but sometimes I turn him around and cum on his tits and in his mouth. I pound him till his clit shoots a big squirt. We meet up as often as he can get away. He has been becoming more and more like a girl when he arrives. Wants to start wearing a wig and wanting to have plugs in his ass all day long so it feels like my cock in him.

There are more and more guys dressing up at the arcades and porn theater. Yesterday there were two guys in different cars getting dressed outside in their cars putting on dresses, stockings, high heals and more. Both driving pickup trucks and wedding rings. This trend is much more open than ever before. I am not seeing cross-dressing with wives as much as I would think. Years ago I would occasionally see guys dressed up as females with their wives but this has not been the case lately. I think more and more guys are living out the fantasy without their wives. And after talking to a few of them there has been a common theme that they were afraid of truly letting their female side show as much as they do when they are alone. Basically embarrassed by how far they take the fantasy. The guys are truly converting to females in actions, dress, voice and how they service men. They come lubed and ready for action.

Many men that I know treat them like females, almost going through the fantasy equally. They think they are truly with a lady. But they get to live out the fantasy and do things to the lady (cross-dresser) that they would never get the chance to do to their wives. And ass fucking is one of the things that truly turn them on, they can't get their wife to consider it so the fantasy lets it happen. And honestly the fake titties that are so realistic only adds to the excitement. When guys bend over and the tits are there to hold while fucking them makes the excitement even deeper.

The amount of money spent on crossdressing is extreme. Hundreds if not thousand of dollars are spent to carry out a fantasy to to ultimate experience. The female experience is also for the guys that are not ready for a physical transition but want the feel of it with out the surgery. Not only is it less costly it also is not permanent if they find out it is not for them much easier to discard the way of life. My crossdresser is fantastic and it truly does make me want it more and more.

19

THE END OR "A NEW BEGINNING"

In closing I truly hope that if you were ever wondering about your partner I have brought a little clarity to this confusing topic and life changing situation. My advise has been spread throughout the book and should be taken as only a guide to possibly help you get to the bottom of your curiosity. There is no definitive answer to your question but now you know the stories of what the lifestyle is and how people get caught up in the life and the lies. And in many cases I created many more questions than answers to that I am sorry.

And to the Anonymous you can not or should not be anything but yourself. Trying to fit into something you are not, will only cause you heartache and disappointment. And it's hard coming to a situation where you must make a decision. But take it from a lier it is no way to live. The lies you tell others are only dwarfed by the lies you tell yourself. It is hard to be something that you think may be you don't want to be, but being what you are is what you are. As a leopard can't change its spots nor can you change long-term your real self.

You can pretend, you can lie, you can miss lead, but you can never hide from yourself. So as my parting bit of advise not that you, asked stop lying, it will be the hardest thing you have ever done but once you become honest you will finally be who you are. Nothing more nothing less, just you! You are not to be put on a pedestal for your bravery you don't need special attention and for fuck sake stop thinking you are more important because you are bi, gay, straight or whatever, you are just you, just like everyone else. Bringing attention to yourself and then acting like someone is wrong for paying attention to you is one of the biggest flags of an insecure person. Stop your insecurity because that is all it is, nothing more nothing less.

Once you stop following the crowd in every aspect of your life you can stop condemning others that do not believe the way you do. If your point of difference is not the same as someone else why do you think they are wrong? They are wrong because they disagree? Really and they think you are wrong because you disagree with them. Can you see the pattern here let's all agree to listen to each other and be friends no matter what because we only have one chance at getting through this world and its always better with friends. Ellen has it right "Be Kind to One Another" Lets start the movement of Understanding, we all can use a little more we can disagree to disagree but once we draw the line in the sand, we may just find all the great understanding lies on the other side of the line.

Enjoy your life to the fullest, work hard, love your neighbors, be kind to all, and life will give you more than you can ever imagine.

Thanks for reading and the support of this journey hope you find comfort and understanding.

Ron (No Longer Anonymous)

AUTHORS BIO

Ron Garrett was born and raised in the Joliet Illinois area an only child. A graduate from Joliet Junior College in Culinary Arts. And a Bachelors degree from Florida International University in Hospitality Management, Miami Florida. Prior owner of multiple restaurant concepts and Corporate Chef of two different food service companies for over twenty five years. Lived in Quad Cities on both Illinois and Iowa side of the Mississippi River. Then moved to Puerto Vallarta, Mexico for over five years after that Fort Lauderdale FL, Wilton Manors area and finally now live in Knoxville TN. Have one daughter and two grandsons in Knoxville. Married two times to women for a total of almost forty years. And during all of the marriage times was bi sexually without either of the wives knowing.